BRYNDIS

A.N. FREDERICK

BRYNDIS

CONTENTS

PLAYLIST

Chapter 1- Wildflower by: Billie Eilish
Chapter 2- Anchor by: Sophia Black
Chapter 3- I fall apart by: Memyselfandvi
Chapter 4- Feral by: Bad Omens
Chapter 5- Daisy by: Ashnikko
Chapter 6- Code Mistake by: CORPSE & Bring me the horizon
Chapter 7- You belong to me by: Cat Pierce
Chapter 8- Always forever by: Cults
chapter 9- Now or never by: Halsey
Chapter 10- Come undone by: Bad Omens
Chapter 11- Fall for me by: Sleep Token
Chapter 12- Blood by: Bad omens
Chapter 13- Heart shaped box by: Neovaii
Chapter 14- The feels by: Labrinth
Chapter 15- Black out days by: Phantogram
Chapter 16- Daydreams by: We Three
Chapter 17- I am not a woman I'm a god by: Halsey
Chapter 18- Seven nation army by: Stevie Howie
Chapter 19- Limits by: Bad Omens
Chapter 20- Pushing daisies by: Neck Deep
Chapter 21- Eat your young by:Hozier
Chapter 22- Okay by:Chase Atlantic

DEDICATION

To the version of me that thought she wasn't good enough, you are.
And to any woman out there feeling the same, you deserve your happy ending too.

TRIGGER WARNINGS

Initially I wasn't going to add warnings to the book and then realized many a person could most definitely be triggered by the content within these pages. Bryndis contains mature themes intended for adult audiences. Triggering content includes themes of alcoholism, sexual assault, kidnapping, human trafficking, murder and genocide. There is also some strong language within these pages so if that's something you aren't comfortable with, feel free to stop reading here. Please take care of your mental health first, always. That being said this book is a wild ride and nothing is truly as it seems. For those that continue, I hope you love it as much as I do.

-A

DEMONS FOR DUMMIES

In the beginning there was us. A slew of humans trying their best to survive in what many deemed to be a wasteland. The bowl like planet we were living on only hospitable on the outskirts, the center of our world nothing but untamed bog lands. We thought we had everything figured out. We were progressing toward being a well-made civilization with a group of royalty at our center leading us to a better world, until The Rift opened. Lucifer and his hoard came flooding through, destroying everything in their path, killing thousands and ending the progress we had so shakily made toward the brighter future we were promised. Nothing could have prepared us for the apocalypse we faced. The leaders of the hoards controlling the very elements around them, molding our world to fit their needs and casting us out in the process. Men could not rise, but we could survive. Thanks to our leadership, that's exactly what we did.

CHAPTER 1

"**B**ryndis, you can't just keep doing your embroidery on the way to class and expect to keep skating by unnoticed," Libby said, her mop of deep brown curls bouncing into her eyes as we walk. She distractedly loops a chain of tiny daisies from the path together, making a full circlet of flowers.

"Well, it's either keep it up or fail completely and then where does that put me?" I huff at her as I stab myself with the stupid needle yet again. Every spare second of my life goes to managing my aunt's estate, which just translates to me being her personal maid. She refuses to move into a smaller home but seeing as the demons seem to be getting closer and closer again, I doubt she'll have ownership of it much longer. Having to do all the work she's too frail for however, leaves me no time to focus on the work for the women's "necessary" curriculum.

The surrounding trees on the way to the main square sway in the breeze and are noticeably very sparse. There have always been paths but given the almost complete lack of weapons in our small town, light is all we really have to keep the demons at bay. Especially in an area that was already the middle of nowhere before The Rise. Before the men farthest from the worst of it decided it was their job to rebuild our world and ensure the survival of the human race. Obviously out of the goodness of their hearts, definitely not because of greed and lust for power. Men could never be so easily corrupted. I thought to myself sarcastically.

We walk the rest of the way to our school, if you can even really call that, in awkward silence. Since The Rift opened and demons came pouring into our realm, schools are nothing more than a hodgepodge of the kids that are left and whoever is able to teach, conglomerated in the largest building in the town that's still standing. It's really all we know at this point. Those who could remember before The Rise were mostly dead and the few that weren't didn't have much insight. Men learn to fight; Women learn just about everything else. As far as the handbook is concerned men are only good for fighting off the hoards, leaving the women to run everything the leaders have deemed integral but overall unimportant. Something to keep our sweet docile minds busy, so they didn't end up with a revolt on their hands. My father always talked about the corruption in our leadership and the injustices regularly doled out in the name of survival before. Clearly, an apocalypse didn't change much.

I would take a class wielding a sword over sewing any day but that's 'not the way of things' as I've been told time and time again. Even with our dwindling numbers we've been well assured that each cog has a part in the bigger system and should one of those pieces get gummed up? There's always a new flow of the next generation to replace them. There is no room for error, no deviation, no difference. Just perfect pretty soldiers to build their empire or breed more people to support it. Knowing that, it doesn't sit well that I've never fit in much with the girls in my year. It's not even just the girls really, I haven't been able to find a place anywhere.

They're small and delicate where I'm tall and curvy. My shoulders rival my hips which roll in a perfect hourglass. My eyes are slightly mismatched, an ocean with a small brown island in my right eye. These days my face seemed to stay constantly scrunched in anger unless it was directed at my tiny, sweet friend who was the only person able to make me feel safe enough to soften the hard exterior I work so hard to upkeep. I keep my black hair long and braided back for functionality and ever since my father's disappearance I've started to use the non-edible berries from the trees skirting the estate to dye the tips crimson the best I can. The closest thing I can get to an actual public act of defiance without ending up carted to wherever it is their prisoners keep disappearing to.

My father spent my entire life stressing the importance of speed after my mother was eaten during the initial wave when I was five, so every day we would run, constantly trying to beat our time from the day before. He taught me to hunt and to forage and climb trees to hide in the foliage. When he was imprisoned, I was only twelve and taught myself to throw his set of knives in a desperate attempt to have some form of self-defense. It felt like even when I wasn't running the sprint never stopped. No one would describe me as elegant, or graceful, or agreeable, so most also didn't bother describing me as a girl. 'It' seems to suffice. To everyone but her.

"You know I wasn't trying to hurt you right, Bryn?" Libby said, peering up at me with her doe shaped honey eyes. She slowly reached up, in an attempt to plop the flower crown on my head like she had a million times before and I bent slightly to accept her roundabout apology. She's smaller than anyone I know, including a handful of the few children in our town. Libby looks more like a fairy than a woman, the crown of her head barely coming up to the base of my sternum. Her mother died last year. She refuses to speak of it, and she's never known her father, so she's spent her time living alone in her mother's yurt on the outskirts of the forests; refusing to even come stay with me at Edna's, which in some ways was understandable. The pair had only settled about seven years prior to her mother's death and given the state of the world all she really had left was her home with its colorful overgrown herb garden lining the entrance.

"I know Liberty, I just don't see what choice I have. I don't particularly want to find out what's on the other side of those," I said gesturing to the beat-up cell on wheels kept right outside the school building as a deterrent, flanked by two imperial guards. Their completely black uniforms almost sucking in the surrounding light. "Watching my father roll away in one was enough." I stop the memory before it can start, like I do every day passing the wagon.

"They say its rehabilitation for the areas you struggle in." She put extra emphasis on the rehab part of her statement, but if it was a rehabilitation center the prisons wouldn't always be empty, the prisoners magically disappearing into thin air once the appropriate amount of time had passed for enough people to forget about them. The makeshift prisons near town at least were never filled.

"Yeah, they say a lot of things," I say rolling my eyes as we turn into the cement building. It had been a community center before and was the only building from the main town that survived the hoards. Half of it has crumbled, and the floor always seems to collect dust and debris no matter how much its swept. There are rooms lining a hall to the left that I assume used to be offices, now being used for makeshift home Ec. classes; to the right is the main meeting room and through the back is the track, that's really just a crater of dirt at this point. That's where those blessed with a penis meet to pummel each other to a pulp.

I get to sit inside and learn how to clumsily embroider my future partners name into their underwear, because apparently accidentally using another mans 'ball hammock' is a huge concern in the barracks. I don't even look toward the back door anymore, no sense in wishing for something that will never be, I'm strong enough and have somehow managed to keep my father's throwing knives, even though me even breathing on them is a criminal offense.

I follow Libby through the door to the right into the large open room for our first class. The only class required to be taken by everyone in the village. The room is covered wall-to-wall in chalkboards haphazardly bolted up and has all twelve men, women and kids in first years in the town bunched around tables facing the front where Professor Sanford has a particularly nasty demon drawn out.

"I don't understand why we need this class," Libby complained, pinching her freckled nose up in distaste at the startlingly realistic drawing as we take our seat closer to the front board.

"So, you know what to watch for and when to run?" I shrug at her, laughing in response.

"If I saw that thing coming toward me, I promise I'd run, with or without instruction." She shook her head causing the crystals woven into her curls to clatter.

"Then you'd be dead," Kallum sneered from the table behind us. "Everyone knows those monsters have instincts only triggered by the hunt. IE you run you die." He finished with a humph. Libby rolled her eyes, and gave me a look, face flushing bright pink in anger.

"He's right," I whisper to her with a sympathetic look as the professor takes his place to share the meager information he has on this creature. I can't help myself as I glance back at the boy I had once loved as a young girl. Kallum, a boy no longer, was now a hulking brute with cool blonde hair that reflected almost silver in the light and deep green eyes that held nothing but anger. He still has a deep scar running the right side of his face, just below his cheekbone that I gave him when we were teenagers. He's made it abundantly clear for the last almost two decades that he has no real interest in a woman not so lovingly nicknamed 'The Ogre' and that likely no one ever would. I can't stop the glare from scrunching my features up further as I take in his massive form behind us, angry with the knowledge that he wasn't even wrong. Outside of dropping Libby off every day and getting a firm squish to the midsection, I don't remember the last time someone hugged me. Definitely never a boy, not since my father's imprisonment. How sad, I think to myself.

His sneer intensifies when he meets my gaze, completely lost in thought. I quickly turn around to pay attention to the demon that was apparently seen on the outskirts of my village. They really are getting closer. I look over at Libby out of the corner of my eye. Her frail shoulders were trembling at the idea of something so deadly being so close to her home.

I take my time memorizing every feature, the way it's snout droops and the loose bands of skin around its midsection, the beady, barely there eyes. It looks no better than one of the rabid dogs not uncommon after The Rise. The bands of skin on its torso were a defense mechanism full of acids that would kill a predator should they be cut open, so avoid those at all costs. It's just one of many I've added into my mental catalog. This one is at least killable if you go for the head. Looking back at Libby, I give her a half smile. She's safe with me, I won't let anything happen to her. I won't lose anyone else.

CHAPTER 2

The rest of the day went by as usual, the rest of the week did really. Wake, pick up Libby, classes, drop Libby off, try desperately to clean a 10-bedroom estate single-handed while my geriatric aunt Edna gripes at me from her sitting room, Bed, Repeat. She always said she wanted her home to be a reflection of heaven and her home was sure a reflection of something; namely anyone who entered. Anything that could be gold was. The floor, the accents, the light fixtures, everything down to the cutlery in her cabinets. Each object in her home was either plush, reflective or both and almost all of it needed to be buffed daily as cleanliness was closest to godliness. She made sure my hands were never idle 'lest the evil take root.' The quirky old woman stuck in the time before The Rise when our greatest worries were what others were doing with their bodies.

After the last demon sighting, I approached Professor Sanford to ask about books or really anything he could offer up to give me an edge. The elderly man was about as frazzled as he always looks. His thinning gray hair puffed up every which way to emphasize his erratic movements as he drew diagrams of demons across the black boards lining the walls of his class. His back is hunched forward, as if the dust itself is pulling him back down to join it. He refused, knowing that getting caught giving me those books would be a death sentence but offered to take me on as an apprentice. If I could help him with sorting through the collections of books he's managed to rescue over the years, I could read and copy down any of the knowledge I deemed useful. Just until we leave for The Summit. This job little more than another thing to add to my ever growing responsibilities.

The days become even more tedious. Each day I stay after classes to help the professor go through his old tomes to make sure the writing wasn't smudged, and they were safely and securely packed for storage. Looking through them meant I got to read each one in its entirety. I worked diligently, transferring the things I thought were important to a small leather-bound notebook. We only actually had two teachers, and the stout woman who teaches 'life skills' is not someone I ever care to think about, nor is she someone who would have anything helpful to offer. The task at hand showed me just how unqualified they truly are to be teaching. This man was a genius but a genius in the arts not in demon lore. Not only did he have nearly no knowledge; the issued 'demons for dummies' books, as father lovingly called them, and the curriculum for women's education that came in after The Rise are barely fifty pages long and don't include some of the demons we'd been taught about. Turns out the professor, in his forties at the time, took it upon himself to find his own research by traveling town to town in the early years after The Rift opened, the old man trying to learn everything he could to survive this.

We were being set up to fail in a system that didn't make sense. A system in which we were only given the illusion of the tools we need to keep us safe when really, we are at the mercy of the cosmos. I didn't realize just how little we knew about them. Before this I was delusional enough to consider myself well-educated and compared to my peers I suppose I am. We have nothing more than an idea as to how to kill some and which ones won't kill you for running. You would think after nearly fifteen years someone would have figured something out; maybe someone did, and we just have no way in our fold of the world to get the information, not past what the professor has been able to find. Maybe my father was right, and we were purposely being kept blind. All I've gleaned from the reading I've been able to do is that there's nothing one can do and no way to avoid the demons, so one must pray to whatever one believes in that you don't stumble upon any of the deadly creatures in the first place. Fantastic.

The days start to drag and a lot of that is fear, existential dread covers nearly every aspect of my life. I'm very near my twentieth birthday which is apparently considered prime time for breeding. This summer, all men and women twenty years of age will be matched at The Summit according to probability of stronger genes, as they have been every year for the last ten years since our 'government' was reestablished. The basic instruction for getting to the center of the kingdom at the forefront of both the men and women's curriculum. It would be foolish of me to think that Libby and I would be top contenders for matches. I've never heard of someone not receiving a match, granted those that left never tended to come back, but the elders have alluded to people rebelling against the great ruler's choices and getting sent straight to the chopping block, partners included for no other reason than convenience.

Maybe it's just me but I don't think it sounds very pleasant to be stuck with a man I've met one time for the rest of my life. I don't know that it sounds fun to be with any man for the rest of my life. Not any of the ones I've met anyway. I had been considering if a life in the woods as a recluse would be all that bad, but sweet Liberty with her trinkets and rambling thoughts wouldn't be able to live a life in hiding happily. So, we make the plans to go. wherever Libby goes I go. She has been very insistent on how fun going on an actual journey together will be which makes our planning a little less daunting. The idea of trouncing the woods with my best friend trumping my fear of the unknown.

Even with the excitement of traveling the gently sloping land with my friend, all my newfound information doesn't make the idea of traveling through the woods unguarded look all that appealing. I've been fairly capable of ignoring it for the most part, but with The Summit only being two weeks away now, I can't keep pretending it's just not going to happen. As I'm wrapping up the last bundle of books the professor had collected, I hear him shuffle up behind me. Instead of taking the books and leaving like he usually would, he sets them to the side and pulls out a small cloth wrapped bundle.

"Never let anyone see this," His gravelly voice rattled as he looked into my soul with his glazed milky eyes. "If anyone does, you didn't get it from me. Everyone deserves a chance." The bite of his breath assaulted my nostrils as he pressed the package into my hands with a small pat, grabbed his books and left, with no more of a goodbye before we were set to leave.

I start the walk back to Aunt Edna's by myself in silence, my heart in my throat. The package, still wrapped, tucked into my bag. Our town is really nothing at this point. The only adults left are those who survived the initial raids but were too old to be matched and a slew of kids of varying ages. Not many people choose to settle here, as we are only about a day from the main rift and in turn were hit hard enough to knock us back to the eighteenth century. The main square is just the school in the middle of a clearing full of debris mountains from buildings that crumbled but were still too big to move. We did the best we could, planting flowers in the crater at the heart of where the town square once was. The brightly colored wildflowers contrasting the destruction even fifteen years couldn't erase.

I don't take a real breath all the way through the woods until I walk through the ornate golden gates of Edna's drive. I don't like traveling this close to dark by myself, even without contraband. I go in as quietly as I can, not wanting to have to do any more 'favors' before I leave for possible death in the morning. Safely tucked away in the first room next to the entry that I've called a bedroom for the entirety of my teenage years, I pull out the bundle of cloth to find a beautiful dagger tucked inside. It was clearly well-loved, polished to a shine, with an ornate hilt and an emerald in the pommel. He was trying to give me a chance to live.

Tears blur my eyes as I stare down at the small backpack I've packed for travel. I look at the bare bones room around me with nothing more than a bed covered by a tattered gray blanket and a chest for my clothes. No personal belongings, no sign I was ever even here. I don't even want to attempt this trek, there are just no other options. I'm so sick of being backed into corner after corner, letting life just happen to me instead of being an active participant. Laying down on my bed, I close my eyes as my thoughts swirl on the hopeless situation be-

.fore me. I take some deep breaths attempting to calm the anxiety trying to flood my system and fall into a fitful sleep, my dreams haunted by beady eyes and the sounds of screams.

When I open my eyes again it's the next morning. I sit up disoriented and try to come up with some sort of plan, but I have absolutely nothing. It'll take us the full two weeks to get where were going on foot and while I know my way around the forests, I've never been on such a long journey. Especially not one with my best friend who hasn't left the village since she settled here. There was a knock on the gold flaked oak door that rung through the entryway as Libby arrived to face our doom together. We smiled tentatively at each other as I looked over to Aunt Edna asleep in her armchair, taking her tiny frame in one last time. A small trail of drool hung from her decrepit face, her severe white bun pulling the wrinkles of her eyes back slightly; The only evidence of life the slight rising and falling of her chest. We've never had much of a relationship outside of survival for us both, but there's a part of me that will miss the old bat and her golden house. Once we leave there's no telling if I'll ever be able to come back, or if this place will still be standing when I do. Taking one last glance at the gaudy interior I've called home the last eight years; I take the first harrowing steps to our future with the closest thing I've ever known to a sister.

CHAPTER 3

It shouldn't have been a hard to make it through the woods, but the farther in we traveled the more I realized that I don't know where we are supposed to be going. It only took a few days before we were officially past where I had ever ventured, and I was relying almost exclusively on the extremely thin bands of people our age migrating in the same direction. No one bothered to give either of us a map outside of a general idea for the capital, and I was starting to get worried that was a purposeful move, so we wouldn't make it. I probably could have torn a page out of one of the books but at that point it would be contraband and I didn't want to risk getting caught because of something so stupid when I was loaded up with weapons I definitely shouldn't have.

"Are you sure we should keep stopping like this?" I ask as Libby kneels to scoop up yet another rock, her sage green skirt billowing around her as she knelt. "We're going to lose the crowd." I look toward the last remnants of people ahead of us, wringing my fingers together. It's hard for me to tell Liberty no; and every oddly shaped acorn, shiny rock, tiny flower, twig arranged just so and even sometimes a toad had to go into her pocket, which happened to set us behind quite a bit.

"Of course. We can still see them, just farther ahead. You worry too much, Bryn." She waved her hand as she giggled at me, standing, content with her spoils.

"I don't think you worry enough, Libby," I say starting to get a little concerned for her mental well-being. "Professor Sanford's classes were nothing. I told you everything I found, and we both know it doesn't span a quarter of what's out there." I point like a crazy person out into the woods, hand shaking. "We don't even really know how our government works or how these matches are truly decided, we've never even met anyone that's been to one of these Summits Libby. That's not weird to you?" I'm definitely starting to panic.

"I feel like we aren't talking about travel anymore." She stops, reaching up to tug at my hand to slow me to a halt too. "I know there's a lot of what ifs. I know things are scary. I see the proof around us every day, but we need to look on the bright side of things," She starts.

"They didn't even give us a map," I nearly whisper.

"I refuse to believe that everything in this world is inherently evil. That must have been an oversight." She nods firmly, giving me a look but I think we both know it was no oversight. We were sent off to take our chances. "Listen, even if we have to make a break for it in the end, or we get hopelessly lost in these woods, I got to go on an epic adventure with my favorite person in the world. And look at all my treasures!" she squeals holding her pocket open to show off the array of trinkets. "Even if what comes is bad, now isn't bad, Bryn. Can we just take this happiness while we have it?" she asks softly. She knows; She is more than aware we're probably not making it to The Summit. I soften immediately.

"Of course, lead on oh great queen of tiny things." I give her a sweeping embellished bow causing her to snort with laughter as she walked on.

The farther in we went the denser the trees were getting; something didn't feel right. The sun was starting to set, and I realized I didn't see any travelers anymore. It was just us on a mostly open path headed in the last general direction I saw people. I look over at Libby, Should I tell her that I have no idea where we are? I don't want to scare her, but I am starting to panic all over again. I'm not concerned about food or the travel, I spent most of my life in the woods skirting our town with my father. I'm a forager, but a bunch of edible plants and the ability to snare a rabbit won't do much good in fighting off a demon or navigating to the heart of our kingdom to be matched. The anxiety gives way to rage. Every single person in our lives and not a single one cared if we made it out of this? Fuck the professor and his knife, we need a map.

Regardless, we can't travel in the dark. I have no way of keeping us safe with a dagger and three warped throwing knives. We decide to stop to set up camp, Libby managing to set a fire like she had for the past six days while I went in search of food. I spent longer than I would have liked finding and skinning a rabbit, so she wouldn't have to watch the worst of the preparation. The time away at least led me to a brook we could come back to, to wash our clothes in and refill our water skins. There were even some wild blueberries on a bush near the rim of the forest leading to the brook. Happily plopping the berries into the satchel I carry on my belt for just this occasion, I merrily started back; swinging our dinner in hand, humming the tune of one of my favorite songs my father used to sing when we would head home from a hunt.

I must have made it most of the way back to camp, I could see the smoke from the fire not far in the distance, the only sure-fire way for me to find Libby again in the denser wood. The crunch of leaves directly next to me halted my humming.

"Hello?" I called out to the trees. There was nothing that I could see, it must have been a squirrel, or another much luckier rabbit. Just as I set out again toward camp, this time making myself as silent as possible, there was another crunch. This one much farther ahead. It's either two separate animals or whatever it is, is moving fast. It was too much closer to where Libby was waiting, where the smoke was coming from.

How could I have been so stupid leaving her openly exposed like that? I freeze, my heart jack hammering out of my chest. I should be running but I can't move a muscle as I try to calm myself. It could be nothing. It is nothing, Bryn. You're just scared because you're lost in the woods, alone, at night. That's a perfectly logical response to...

My thoughts are abruptly cut off not by a crunch but this time by a scream I would have recognized anywhere.

"LIBERTY!" I roar racing through the woods toward the only person I have left that loves me. Branches slap my face and rip strands of hair from my braid as I run, pushing my legs faster than they've ever gone.

"LIBBY!" I call again, the forest a blur around me, practically flying over the ground under my feet. Praying to anything out there that she'll respond and that I've worked myself into a tizzy for no reason; but she doesn't respond, and when I finally make sense of my surroundings, I realize I'm back at our camp. The same open field I left her in, with a fire blazing in an opening between two trees at the edge. Her embroidery hoop is sitting next to the fire, her pack slumped against the same tree it was when I left but no Libby.

I frantically start scanning the field but there isn't a single thing out of place. My brain completely shuts down. There's no thought, no plan, no emotion. Just absolute emptiness. I don't even realize that I've crossed our camp to where Libby's project lay discarded on the ground until I pick it up. I run my fingers over the dainty flowers embroidered into the edge of a handkerchief, daisies, and underneath of them my name only missing the 's'. My heart splinters, she had nothing to defend herself with. Nothing but an embroidery needle that was now glistening from the ground with specks of blood on it. My ears start ringing as I fall to my knees. My best friend is dead, she must be. The demon must have gobbled her up in one bite and took off before I could get back. So much for speed, Bryn.

Tears fill my eyes and I curl up on my side facing the fire as it slowly dies. Everyone always dies on me; it was foolish of me to ever think I could keep either of us safe. I'm stuck in a forest obviously prowling with demons. I have no map, and there are no signs of life anywhere near me. The odds couldn't be more laughable. I don't even want to try to rage against them, I just want a break. I just want to breathe for a second. I just want to stop running.

***

I spend two days nearly comatose, making a single skin of water and the berries from the pouch I had initially grabbed for Libby stretch. I have no idea where to go or what I'm supposed to do in this situation. I have yet to see anyone on the road again, So I lay, staring at the needle still in the dirt; trying to figure out what could have possibly happened.

I can barely even find the will to sit up, but my thoughts never stop turning. Wondering if she was hurt badly or if she would resent me for giving up so easily. If the roles were reversed, would she not have done better? Wouldn't she have looked for me? Refusing to believe anything but her happy ending.

I know my speed; I need to know how far the brook was from here to know how long it took me to get back. I finally arise from my little meltdown and decide that if I have no idea where to go, I'm going to make my own way, enough of being helpless. If I'm going to die it'll be on my own terms. I head back toward the brook and find it within half an hour. Looking over the water I fish through my pack and pull out my minuscule notebook of demon information. Staring down at the worn leather one last time, I chuck it into the brook, the information useless to me. I take some time and wash my clothes, bathe and allow myself a second to regroup. So much has happened in the last few weeks, and I have no way of processing any of it. There's no room left in me to be afraid, at least now the only thing I stand to lose is my own life.

Drying off on the bank I think over my brief hike here. It couldn't have taken me longer than seven minutes at a full sprint from here to get back to her, and I was much closer than that so how did they disappear without a trace? Demons will usually eat a person but it's not uncommon for them to take one either, although no one really knows why. Should it have eaten her there would be at least some evidence. Nothing big enough to swallow her whole would have made it through without me seeing it. It had to be something small, and I guess it makes sense, it wouldn't have been able to take me but Libby? She would have been the perfect target for something like that to snatch. It stands to reason that Liberty very well could be alive, and if she's out there somewhere, I'm going to find her; even if it kills me in the process.

CHAPTER 4

I hike back from the brook to scan the field of our camp closer, thankful no other soul has passed through. I spend a good chunk of time pacing the outskirts trying to find anything that could give me a sign of which direction to go, when I see it. A sapling trampled right over; it couldn't have come higher than my ankle before being crushed. We didn't come from this way.

The odds are likely this is a false lead but it's all I have. I start tracing bits of carnage through the shaded canopy of the trees, treating this the same as hunting. I walk for hours and eventually the trampled foliage stops as the layer of leaves starts to become more spongey and goopy. I've easily been walking half the day deeper and deeper into the dark never even looking up from the ground for signs of my friend. I come up on a tree that looked like a demon traveling through had scraped their horns through the bark. The trunk so eaten into, a strong gust of wind would probably topple the tree. I keep walking but I can't see anything else to follow. The sunlight barely filters through the leaves now, the light choked out by the dense foliage. I have to find her and fast.

I stop to sit down for a second and catch my breath. The sun is fully setting now and tongues of fire dance through the leaves as the light shifts. The golden glint filtering through the canopy overhead catching on something shiny back a few paces, at the base of the mutilated tree. It was a crystal, an amethyst she loved and always kept woven into the front section of her hair. I pick it up, holding it tight. Proof that her body at least made it this far. I don't want to make a camp, but the dark is settling in quickly and the insects around me are taking up their nightly choir.

I can't risk starting a fire so deep in the bog lands, so I decide to climb a tree and sleep where the two thickest branches meet. I didn't ever really fall asleep though; just sat there holding that amethyst and watching the light slowly change through the leaves until dawn had broken enough for me to travel again. Not a sound around me out of place.

I start back in the direction I spent the entire last day heading in. From here all I see are signs of Libby.

Every so often I'll find a crystal, an acorn, a daisy, things that couldn't have come out of this bog, always at very weird angles throughout the path. Almost like her trinkets were being dropped from the sky. I follow the trail, my heart breaking with every piece I find. She was emptying her pockets leaving me a trail to her and I spent two days laying in a patch of dirt? She deserves a better friend than me, I wouldn't blame her for agreeing wherever she is.

My feet are starting to stick in places as I travel deeper into the bog. It's not long before all trail cuts off and the trees have smothered all the light. I can barely see, my only saving grace was the gradual decline of light naturally adjusting my eyes. I haven't even turned a full circle to take stock of where I am when there's a massive thud, followed by the deepest chuckle I've ever heard directly behind me.

"Looks like someone's a little lost." That insanely deep accented timber sounds from right behind me.

Gripping my dagger that I had been keeping tucked into my belt, I spin in a flash catching him by surprise. The blade skimming the broad expanse of a burgundy abdomen. Not him, it.

The demon was massive. It towered over me, forcing me to crane my neck to see its face which looked absolutely pissed. Its pug like snout scrunched up, further narrowing its almost glowing yellow eyes and showing six-inch-long fangs sharper than any dagger I owned.

"Oi, didn't ya mum teach ya any manners?" He snorts down at me, blowing my braid back. My breath hitches. My blade did absolutely nothing and if I wasn't mistaken this was only essentially a grunt. I am so fucked.

Wide eyed I scramble back hitting trees on the way. As I scurry, I get a glimpse of his entire torso, covered in swirling black ink. His huge horn topped mottled wings peeking up over his shoulders. He strides toward me and I close my eyes, tripping over the vines under my feet. Falling to the ground I clutch my dagger and mentally apologize to Libby for not being able to save her when I hear a set of chains. That's weird. My confusion deepens as I'm promptly lifted by hands the size of my torso. He holds me by my biceps, setting me gently back onto my feet.

Slowly I peeked open one eye, taking in the good old fashion manacles now on my wrists. My eyes flung open as he plucked the dagger, barely the size of his fingernail, from my hands and stood back to casually stand in front of me like this is an everyday occurrence for him. I couldn't think of a single thing to do as I stood before him chained, mouth agape, trying to understand why this monster is just standing there looking at me like my confusion is offensive.

"Ya got sumthin to say en say it." He all but growled down at me.

"You're not going to kill me?" It's the only question that popped into my blank head, the adrenaline coursing through me leaving nothing but silence in my brain.

My mental capacities are officially burnt out from having to make so many adjustments to my thought process in a matter of days; it feels like it should have been months.

"ya humans always assumin we're out here to eat and kill and maim but really some of us are just out here tryin to make an honest living, Doll." Doll? Is this thing for real? I scoff and the demons face loosens, eyebrows shooting up to almost touch the massive horns sticking out of his head like an ox. I've been dealing with condescending men since I took my first breath, this one isn't special.

"And the chains?" I ask confident I won't be dying anytime soon. He officially doesn't look angry anymore, just amused by my clear lack of sanity.

"Silly Lui." He seemed to murmur to himself. "My livin is sellin' dames like you. We don't only breed with demons and the demand is much higher than the supply if ya catch my drift. There's good coin out there for someone that can do the job, but for one so small and pretty? Priceless." He licked at his snout as he unfolded his wings. He walked around me, gingerly putting the dagger back in my pack, clearly not worried about me having a weapon.

This is worse than being eaten, this is so much worse. The demon grabbed me, cradling me into his massive chest as he made to take off like I was the most precious thing he ever carried, and for the first time in a very long time I felt small.

CHAPTER 5

He kept me cradled in his arms as he quickly flew just above the tree line. The wind is tearing the water from my eyes but I'm not about to close them and miss where he's taking me. He found me fairly early in the morning, and judging by way the sun was angled in the sky we had been flying for hours in complete silence. I could still see the ground below peeking through the trees. Maybe that's why Libby's trinkets were so sporadic, could she have been carried by a similar creature?

"Soooo, Lui?" I brave glancing up at him to nothing by an eye full of razor-sharp teeth. I quickly glance back toward the ground; the height is less scary than what's holding me.

"Is that like short for anything or?" In that moment I realize how little of my sanity remained, and realistically exactly why me and Libby were friends. Most women probably wouldn't be talking to their captor, let alone a massive demon but I'm hoping maybe humanizing him will make this experience less terrifying. At least we know I can still get scared. I think to myself grimly, rolling my eyes at my own idiocy running directly into the bog.

"Yeah, Lucifer." He chuckles as my eyes turn into saucers looking back up at him and meeting amused glowing eyes. Now that I'm closer I realize they're golden, like the floors in Aunt Edna's house.

"Like... wait Lucifer like... The..."

"Yeah." He cuts me off. "Me mum was a fan." He mumbles back like it's an embarrassment. Demons are so much weirder than I anticipated. I've never seen this kind of demon before, he just matched the few descriptions of their races foot soldiers. When we were learning about Lucifers rising, this demon was exactly what I pictured. The one who brought the initial hordes of mindless creatures flooding through The Rift, clearly this wasn't the same guy though. How many of them are there? I can't for the life of me focus my thoughts, they're just spinning endlessly.

I spent so many hours studying everything Professor Sanford had on demons to be able to defend us, and I was correct in the assumption that the knowledge we have is nothing. No more than basic information on the demon equivalent of dogs. I doubt if I started asking for demon history Lui would give it to me and even if he would, going into this blind may be the lesser evil.

"Am I the first girl you've taken from these forests or is this a regular occurrence for you?" I questioned, unable to keep the accusation out of my tone. He huffed, clearly not a question he was willing to answer. What if he carried Libby. He would surely remember her, but I would have to get him to give me actual answers to find out. I sigh and settle deeper into his hold.

I don't know that it's wise to talk to him longer than I have to, when he could easily drop me if I annoy him. He's so odd though. He's been carrying me like I'm the world's most precious cargo and outside of his blatant declaration to sell me he doesn't seem that bad, not beyond his appearance anyway, just a little gruff. I also don't want to meet my doom with nothing but my own thoughts, not with Libby out there, gods know where.

"Lui?" I can justify one more question while we're up here. Just to know who I'm dealing with. "Do you like this? What you do for a living, I mean."

"Course I do," he says gruffly but there's sadness behind his response. Or maybe I'm just looking for reasons to justify his actions, so I'm not completely alone in this.

Lui is starting to slow down and in the distance, I can see large wooden turrets holding together a series of mismatched wooden walls. Like a makeshift village in the heart of the densest part of the bog lands. Lui stiffens as we get closer, he seemed to get bigger if that's even possible. He puffs up his chest becoming infinitely more menacing, like he was trying to put on a show for anyone who may glance up. We come up on a clearing leading to an entryway with a massive wooden gate that's been rolled back to allow non winged patrons inside. It really is exactly what it looks like, a village where demons can walk freely. Lui glances down at me taking in the disheveled state I was in and loops back around to land in the tree cover just beyond the gates entrance.

"What are we doing?" I start to panic again as he slowly lowers to the ground.

"Shining me newest treasure." He chuckles darkly, right before his feet land on the marshy ground just beyond sight of the village.

CHAPTER 6

The second we hit the ground I leap out of Luis arms to start running, because there is absolutely no way I'm going into a keep full of demons. What I didn't consider was the fact that my legs were completely numb from being horizontal for a good day. I hit the ground and I hit hard, face to dirt. There's no way my nose isn't broken, Lui had to be over 8 feet tall. He picked me up by the pack still attached to my back and scrutinized my face.

"Ya earned that one, ya did," he mumbled as he fished a hankie out of his pocket to dab at the blood coming from my nose with clawed fingers. He's wearing pants? Of course, he is. Better question, handkerchief? I stare at him in bewilderment as he cleans up the rest of my face and breaks the band holding my braid in, still hold-ing me by the backpack. I don't even have it in me to protest as he unbinds my hair, using his claws as a brush to make the slightly wavy strands lay flat again. He gin-gerly set me back on my feet with a pat on the head. His few touches are so delicate I can barely feel them, like he's scared if he isn't this gentle with me, I'll break. This is the weirdest thing I've ever experienced in my life.

Lui began herding me across the field, through the gates and into the village where I'm overwhelmed by sights and sounds and smells. The cicadas abruptly cut off as we passed through the wards and the place came alive with chatter and ethereal music I wouldn't mind hearing for the rest of my life. Right as we walk in, I see a group of demons I've never seen before. They looked like Lui but smaller and much more humanoid. As if they were people that had spontaneously grown horns and a set of wings. And a tail? I catch as Lui leads me quickly away from the rows of set up shops, divided by ornate rugs and tapestries, taking me to what looked like a mas-sive stone egg off to the farthest end of the wall that I could see.

There seemed to be a bunch of these massive circular structures lining the walls on the inside of the village, almost like perfect little pods. They looked to have been carved out of boulders. Each egg with a perfectly fit door, and a window directly next to it. I can't say I'm surprised, the few upper-level demons we know of from The Rise had elemental magic. It wouldn't be hard for someone who wields the earth to their advantage to carve a room out of a massive rock.

He gestured me into the space with a huff and shut the door without a word. Little orbs of light float across the ceiling, chasing the shadows away as I took in my surroundings. It was clearly made for a human. A little cot with furs for a blanket sat on the furthest side of the space, a tiny table with a matching rickety chair next to it and a chamber pot directly to the right of the window, score. Once I attended to needs I hadn't in almost full day, I attempted to shimmy my pack off my back while still manacled. I got about halfway to being able to get into it when I realized there were men at the window, just standing there watching me. Not men, Demons? They looked like regular men, but their skin tones were variations of reds, purples, greens; every color really including some that would be naturally found in a human. Some had horns or wings or both.

There were also faceless figures floating behind, too tall for me to see without getting any closer, nothing but lumps of varying colors. Scratch that this is the weirdest thing I've ever experienced. I freeze in place, realizing my shimmying has been giving them a show I know good and well they aren't paying for. Well, paying me for. I just stare at them as they whisper to each other. Some demons moving along just for new ones to join as the former filtered out. In that moment it hits me. I'm for sale. This is a demon market not a village, and this is the pretty packaging I come in, like a pearl in an oyster.

Something in me snaps at the realization, and the rage of having no control over any aspect of my life bubbles up, ready to boil me alive. I pull my pack around the best I can with my hands in front of me, and I dig the dagger out of it. The straps on my arms are making me want to crawl out of my skin. The tiny room is closing in, every layer I'm wearing feels suffocating but I can't do anything with these fucking shackles. I cut the straps off my pack and toss it onto the ground, but that small lack of a layer doesn't do much to quench the boiling rage sitting under my skin, forcing its way out. I flip the cot over and kick its flimsy frame out of the way, and take a second to assess my surroundings before I turn to the doorway to try to force my way out.

Tucking my dagger back into my belt where it belongs, I run for it head on, slamming into the stone door with all my weight. The rock doesn't budge, no matter how hard I shove. My side is definitely going to hurt in the morning. I try my dagger, attempting to stick it into the seam of the door trying to pry it open, but I can't even get the point of my knife into the opening. I scream in frustration and pace across the room toward the table in the corner with a single chair. Getting a good grip into the dagger I put my weight into the throw directly at the window that has now gathered quite an audience. The blade sinks into the window before it just stops, like it was caught in time, hurtling directly at the demons greedily watching beyond.

Of course the window is also warded, if the door is sealed shut. I start putting every ounce of helplessness I feel right now into obliterating this room. If they want to sell me, I'm not going to make it easy for them. I hurl the chair through the air, it smashes into the stone door splintering into some good size shards. I flip the small table causing the face to crack, it's clearly been sitting here for quite some time. Panting I survey my destruction, there's nothing left for me to break, short of the cot. They seemed to have thought this living situation through. I see red as I wonder just how many women lived in here before me.

I will not be bought and transferred from one cage to another like some sort of glorified pet. I'm running out of steam though, the rage quickly trickling into a crushing sadness I don't think I'm prepared to face. My breathing is coming out like choked sobs. Looking back at the window one more time I see the faces practically licking the glass trying to see the moment I realize the situation is helpless, the moment I give up. I lock onto a pair of eyes that look to hold a galaxy in their blackness, baring my teeth in feral rage before giving the finger to every person in my life that had ever forced me into a corner just as small when I was never meant to be caged. To each of these disgusting things fully prepared to buy a living breathing being.

In a final act of defiance, I grab my chamber pot from beside the window, the only area of the room out of view, and step back to hurl it full-force directly at the window. The porcelain shatters as it hits the hilt of the dagger still embedded in the opening. That's exactly what I think of them. The demons very quickly find something better to do with their time. As it turns out, even demons want a woman a little easier to manage. I smirk to myself, until I realize those black eyes stayed, Leaving nothing but a cosmic glint in the complete darkness outside my window. I quickly wrap myself up in the bundle of furs on the floor by my feet and curl up along the back side of the wall, as far from the window as I can get. Sitting there, huddled in a ball, I can't stop thinking of constellations and how I could have sworn it looked like those eyes were smiling.

CHAPTER 7

Every time I do the absolute most to destroy this room, it returns to its original state by morning. This must be some sort of sorcery, I've heard of warding but pure magic? It's not even just what came with the room, when I woke up my nose and side were healed as if nothing happened, the dried blood flaking off my shirt was the only sign I had ever even been injured. Even my pack, propped up in the corner I threw it into, is completely repaired. It's been days of taking my frustrations out on this tiny space, and I've run out of ideas. I'm starting to feel like a meerkat, consistently popping in and out of the furs as man like, and not so man like creatures come to my window. I feel most comfortable sleeping during the day when the figures tend to dwindle, but then I have to deal with the fluctuating demons outside the window once they start prowling the darkness more openly.

There hasn't been a single sign of Lui since he ushered me in and sealed the door shut. It's been just over a week now, and the black eyes seem to consistently come and go. They never get any closer though, never revealing anything but their eyes illuminated by the balls of light that float randomly around my room each night to light the space. It's weird, but those eyes almost make me feel a little safer, like I have some kind of constant in this absolutely awful situation.

I wake up for the night and peek out of my furs. Each day a basket of various fruits and grains will appear sitting nicely on the table that I've broken at least five times now. It's always more than enough to survive on but it's obvious that they're trying to keep their product as transportable and weak as possible. That or their magic is severely limited in what its able to provide. The manacles have started to rub at my wrists, irritating my skin. I sit there and wonder if anyone is in the other huts and who has been here the longest without being bought. If maybe by some miracle Libby is also tucked away inside one of these little cubbies. If whoever purchases me will be like Lui, or like the demons that eat those in the woods found out after dark.

When I'm sure the coast is clear, I quickly grab some apples and a loaf of brown bread from the basket and try to rush back to my bed before anything can catch me unawares. Days of living in the same clothes have taken their toll. My white shirt is starting to yellow slightly and is covered in mud, my blood and gods knows what else at this point, exactly as it was when I entered. I have a spare set of breeches and a camisole, but I had anticipated being able to wash my shirt and the brown lace up vest I wear in the streams along the way and you couldn't pay me to lose layers in a market literally after my body.

I curl back up in my fur nest and realize someone has indeed been watching me. He looks like most of the other demons I've seen but his skin is so pale it almost seems to sparkle, even in the low lighting. I'm so shocked by the sudden appearance of what is surely an angel that I realize I've frozen with an apple still securely between my teeth. Finishing my bite, I pull the furs around me closer, using them as a shield from this creature I can't seem to look away from.

I cock my head, taking him in, narrowing my eyes at his gorgeous visage. He cocked his head in return. His skin was offset by a simple black lace up shirt, and what looked like a swirling tattoo peeking out onto his left collarbone. The angel, sorry demon, had a jaw line that could cut glass covered by the lightest dusting of stubble, and full perfect lips that I didn't really want to look away from. His nose sloped into his strong eyebrows, and his head of curly black hair did nothing to conceal the silver horns looping from his head like a ram. Every inch of them covered in a delicate looping pattern I don't think even the best artist could recreate. He is absolutely devastating. The depictions of our gods fall short in comparison to the creature before me.

Then I noticed his eyes, deeply shadowed and sunken in and so dark when I met them it felt like I was falling into them. Like I could simply drown there and lay happily among the souls he's stolen before me. The entirety of them a black field holding an eternity, if you take the time to really look. Those are the eyes. Oh gods, I threw my chamber pot at him? My face flushes and I realize with a start that I've dropped both the furs and my apple completely into my lap and the chunk I just bit into has just been sitting in my mouth, like I've forgotten all sorts of human function. Sputtering trying to find some way to escape the fact that a creature as gorgeous as that has just been standing here watching me on and off for days, I quickly completely huddle under the furs still clenched in my fist, but not before I finally see the smirk gracing that full set of lips instead of just those abysmal eyes.

***

I spend the rest of the night under my furs and sleep through the day yet again. Why would he keep coming back after seeing all of that. Not even just the first day, but the days after spent flipping tables and smashing the contents of my room to nothing. My dreams are haunted by black pits and perfect lips and the delicate spirals of what is objectively a beautiful set of horns.

When I feel brave enough to emerge, he's still there watching me with those never-ending pits, amongst a smattering of others scoffing and chattering as usual. Has he even moved since I saw him last? He seemed to be in the same spot, but he still looked immaculate. Like he didn't spend twenty-four hours standing outside of a window. It's no surprise to me that Lui is having trouble making the sale. I expected having trouble finding someone of my own species. This constant waiting around for someone to move me to my final resting place is getting tedious and I would give anything just to hear someone speak. Days alone in a room being observed will get to you, I don't know how much longer I can handle being in here without my mind slipping; I mean I'm literally dreaming about a sexy demon, maybe it already has. Speaking of sexy demons, I meet the black eyes of the thing that's been watching me and scowl.

"Is the show really that good?" I sneer at him past the others. My voice comes out hoarse from disuse, and I realize I haven't bothered trying to talk since that first day. I haven't said anything beyond screaming. I haven't even had the chance for a good proper cry yet. The creature eyebrows shoot up, seemingly amazed I had chosen to speak to him. He raises a large hand to his head, and points at his ear with a finger that is slightly too long. He can't hear me. It's silent in here outside of the sound of my breathing. I roll my eyes and throw one of the throwing knives from my pack into the table I've turned on its side to join the other two stuck there. The manacles make the movement clumsy, but it sticks in the wood just like the others. I look back into those inky pools to see a look of absolute wonder cross his beautiful features, before rolling over on my cot to hum one of my dad's old hunting tunes into the silence. We were supposed to be at The Summit now. Happy birthday to me, I think to myself sarcastically as I fall asleep with nothing but my own swirling thoughts.

CHAPTER 8

Something is touching me, everywhere. I'm completely immobilized, it feels like every muscle has been tenderly wrapped up for shipping. I must still be sleeping, wrapped up in the warmth of a galaxy. The scent of mahogany, teakwood and fire is slowly lulling me from my sleep; I tried to roll with a groan as my hip bumps into something hard. My eyes fly open to meet the galaxy I was just dreaming about, the black gaze of him. I'm not dreaming, he is indeed, sitting on the edge of my cot just staring, waiting. If I could move, I would have started thrashing. All I can do is look at him in panic, trying to figure out what is happening. I can't even open my mouth to ask.

"I'm going to release you, but I'm going to need you to be a good girl and stay still or you'll alert the others," he whispers, his rich voice would have made me shiver if my body wasn't completely locked in place. "One blink for yes?"

I blink at him. Eyes rocketing around, trying to wake up. I'm still in my cubby, on my cot and it's light outside. Wait. It's daytime? I really take a second to look at him. The mystery demon from outside my window has added a large black cloak to his get up to add ample shade to his face. His horns were completely covered. He could pass for an ordinary traveler on the road.

"Smashing," he says with a smile that makes my chest ache, and the hold on my muscle's releases. He was doing this. Forcing my body to submit by welding its very essence. His element was water, therefore blood. Terror coursed through me, but in that same second the realization dawned that the manacles had been re-moved. The looping chains now nothing but a heap of metal on the ground beside my bed.

Seeing the opportunity, I grabbed the dagger from under my pillow, and drew up as quickly as I could. His long fingers wrapped around my wrist stopping the dag-ger just as the tip started to dig into the delicate skin under his jaw. He held me there for a moment. In the stillness I watched the single drop of blood run down my knife, over my fingers, and down to his massive palm still holding my wrist. This wasn't hot.

He tsks. "Feeling playful today, are we? I so love a challenge." Before I can even blink, he's moved to hover right over me. His face inches away, baring his teeth still holding my hand and the knife firmly in place. I lose control of my entire body again, but my fingers are locked still firmly clutching the dagger as he removes it from his jaw. The small puncture wound closing before it even had the chance to drip. Looking me dead in the eyes, he licked what was left of the blood droplet from the blade, elongated canines glinting in the light. This wasn't hot.

"I don't mind keeping you at my whim, but it will be much easier to escort you out of here if you walk willingly." He cocks his head as he grins down at me with that damn face of his. I blink an exaggerated blink again. This time he only releases the hold on my legs and feet allowing me to stand.

"I don't make things easier for brats," He says, simply wrapping a muscled arm around my back to put my pack on me after dropping my dagger into it yet again, before he ushers me from the enclosure I was being kept in. It's hard to balance very well without control of your upper half, and it's almost as if he's getting some sort of sick satisfaction watching me struggle and sway trying to keep my bearings. We made it about halfway to the main gate when he scoots me securely into his hold.

"Seems we've been discovered love. Bear with me." His lips brushed the shell of my ear, and even his hold on my blood couldn't stop the shiver that raced down my spine. How long had it been since I'd been touched like that? Never. This is not some hero whisking me off though, he's a demon that's purchased me. Honestly, though? Looking up at him I can't say that I can complain. Not for this moment, for this moment he can be my knight in shining armor.

I feel all my muscles loosen as he breaks his hold over them and I gear up to take off toward the gate and get far away from all of this, when he tosses me over his shoulder like I'm nothing more than a sack of grain. No one in my village ever had the audacity to even try to lift me. Yet here this damn near glittering avenging angel is, running to the gates with me slung over his broad shoulder; a trail of demons running behind. None of them seem to be putting much effort into the chase, but my knight picks up his speed, racing for the gate. Among the demons chasing us was Lui, the biggest of the bunch, putting on quite the show of falling behind his peers, huffing and puffing as he throws a wink my way. I wave at the familiar demon in farewell as we cross the entryway into and out of the city.

Once we were safely out of the market, my knight set me down on the ground again and I couldn't stop the giggle that escaped me. Obsidian eyes turn to me, crinkled in amusement.

"That was fun, though maybe next time I'm saving your life you could cooperate." His smile lit up his entire face. I wasn't imagining it; he was such a stark pale white he glistened, even in the low light filtering through the canopy of trees.

"Saving my life? Is that what it's called when someone takes complete and total control of your body and removes you from your burrow?" I glare at his beautiful face as he chuckles. The sound richer than anything I've ever heard. Butterflies erupt in my stomach, and I quickly set to work smothering each and every one.

"Would you like to go back?" His grin grew as my eyes widened. "You had full function over your legs, and yes saving your life. Nothing decent can afford the price tag on your head." He had this weird way of looking down at me even though he wasn't much bigger. Standing a few paces away it was easy to tell my eyes would be at level with his chin.

"And are you?" I ask, surveying my surroundings, trying to find a way away from him and back the way I came.

"Am I?" He moved closer to me. Every step I took was met with one of his own.

"Decent?" I start as I look back, meeting black eyes that are far closer than I anticipated. He grins again, wide enough for me to fully see his pointed canines and my breath stutters.

"Absolutely not, but it seems a waste to me, getting you all the way here just to let something that had no business touching you, crush you? Such a pretty.... Dove. So fragile. Can't have you breaking." He runs a too long finger gingerly over my cheekbone and down to my collarbone. I swallow. Hard.

"Okay. Then, thank you I suppose." Clearing my throat, I take a large step back from him and look back toward the market, still visible from the tree line where everyone has gone back to life as normal. "Shouldn't they be chasing us?" I turn back toward the stunning creature in front of me.

"Even demons have a code... do you have a name?" He stops abruptly.

"Bryndis." I reply in haste, hoping I'll get the rest of my answer. He smiles at me, the sight as beautiful as the sun breaking through the clouds.

"...Bryndis." He says my name like he's tasting each letter. "If you can take something fast enough, once you're out of the city it's yours. Lui has more product in there than he knows what to do with this time of year, and he owes me one. So, you're with me red," he finishes, reaching up to run his fingers through the dyed ends of my hair that haven't been washed in well over a week now. Every time I step away, he just gets closer.

"Well then, do I get to know my saviors name?" I peer up at him through my eyelashes, the way he takes up all the air surrounding me makes him feel massive.

"Asmodeus," He murmurs, staring at my lips. How am I supposed to get away from him if he keeps looking at me like that. I mean walking toward me. I totally wasn't frozen in place under the weight of his gaze. How could this man have me so flustered?

I take as big a step I can back toward the woods, not wanting my back turned to him, but trying to put some space between us. He sees exactly what I'm doing, and that soul crushing grin lights his face as he prowls closer, step by step. He's playing with me. I tuck a loose strand of hair behind my ear before I abruptly turn but keep my steady retreat into the wooded area; the sound of cicadas filling the air, followed by the heavy crunching of our boots. I slowly start shifting my pack to reach my knife. I have an arm out of my bag now, but there's no way I'm swinging it around and rooting through it without him noticing, but maybe if I use the bag itself, I can knock him out and take off. I swing it forwards and lose my grip on the handle. The straps slip through my fingers and the pack lands with a smack against the muddy ground. Of course, their city is built in the middle of the bog. A bog that my pack and everything I own is sinking into, my body is sinking into really.

Frantically, I plunge my hand into the dirt trying to find my bag. I grab the handle and give a yank, but it seems to be firmly rooted. I could scream. It's not until that chuckle sounds behind me that I do. I scream in rage at everything that has happened to me and everything I stand to lose. Tears fill my eyes, but I refuse to let them fall as I struggle. I pull and twist the strap, but it isn't coming up and the more I struggle the more I'm sinking. I still, deciding that I'd really rather not keep wagging my ass in the face of an ungracious demon.

"Please do keep struggling, I am so enjoying watching you writhe," he says as my movement slows to a stop. I look back at him incredulously under my arm.

"If you don't want me to drown in this, you're going to have to help me out of it," I bite out at him.

"Oh, I'll help you little Dove. But not until you ask nicely." That grin has both my fist and my thighs itching for his face. There's definitely something wrong with me. At this point I'm up past my knees and my arm to my elbow is well and truly stuck but I still have what I'm almost positive is my pack handle. I'm not willing to lose my knives.

"Please, oh dear benevolent Asmodeus, would you unstick me from this sticky situation I have found my-self in." I look at him under my stuck arm, bending far-ther in half to completely meet his eyes and bat my eyelashes at him. He seemed dumbstruck for a moment, glancing between what I assume is my face and my butt as I pout my lip out, dripping sarcasm. He strode forward completely unbothered by the terrain and simply ripped me from the mud mixture, carrying me out of it like a purse, pack and all.

"The next time you're begging me for something it won't be sarcastically I can assure you that." His voice darkened as he continued carrying me by the midsec-tion back the way we came. My toes curled at the promise in his tone before I could stop them. How bad is it really, to be attracted to one's captor? Where on the scale of morally gray does this fall? Do I even care?

He carried me like that all the way back to the spot on the trail I detoured from, which is honestly an embarrassingly short distance, before setting me on my own two feet with a boop to the nose. He had circled us all the way back to the edge of the woods near the demon market.

"Not thinking of returning me already, are you?" I asked, a little scared that's exactly what he was doing.

"Never." His eyes darkened. Stepping closer I could see him sizing me up before he said. "I'm just trying to figure out how to get you home without losing you to the mud." He clearly didn't anticipate me being a very cooperative captive. I can't stop my grin as he stops his pursuit to stare at me, almost like he was open to ideas. I pursed my lips surveying the starts of the bog around us.

"You'd think you'd have thought this through a little better." I try to deadpan but quickly fell into laughter, the shocked look he was giving me melting into a grin.

"I'm sorry I don't make stealing beautiful women a more common occurrence, I'll make sure to more thoroughly think of your comforts, my queen." He laughs and steps forward, quickly sweeping my legs up and catching my back, effectively cradling me into his chest.

"What are you doing?" I gasp worried he'll drop me, but his grin is dazzling as he looks down at me like he could carry me forever.

"Thinking of your comfort."

CHAPTER 9

Asmodeus carried me through the worst of the bog before setting me down on the trail and I quickly bolted, not making it more than five feet before my body locked up refusing to move. "Damn it," I mumble mid stride. He just scooped me right back up, cradling my frozen muscles in his arms and continues on his merry way, humming a tune I couldn't place. I gave him a look mentally and as if he sensed it, my muscles slowly loosened.

The next time he puts me down on the trail to give my legs a break from their mostly seated position I bolt again, this time making it almost out of his eyesight before I, again, lose control of my muscles. I was going much faster this time, and the sudden halt caused me to topple over, getting a face full of marshy dirt. "Damn it," I mumble into the ground. He let me get farther that time. Is this a game to him? Of course it is. He's laughing this time as he scoops me up, tossing me over his shoulder.

The last time I attempt to run, I very cunningly convinced him I needed to attend to my bladder. Ever the gentleman he turned his back and I extremely quietly crept away. I got well into the trees away from where I was supposed to be when I heard crashing, followed by him bellowing my name. My heart panged a little bit at the sound of his panic.

I ran as fast as I could into the woods, not caring about the noise, when I ran smack dab into what felt like a marble pillar. My head spun as I was hurtled to the ground by my own velocity. Taking a second to collect myself I looked up right into the feral grin of Asmodeus. Grabbing me by an arm he hauls me over his shoulder, yet again, this time delivering a firm but not painful smack to my backside as he started walking, and I yelped, face flushing.

"I don't mind chasing you, Dove. You only have to ask." He set me down back on the path before grabbing my chin with his thumb and forefinger, forcing me to look into his eyes. "But if you ever make me think you've been taken from me like that again, your punishment will be far, far worse than a swat." My entire body clenched at the threat in his eyes as he lifted me back up to carry me farther into the nameless woods. I lay draped over his back trying to quell the lava churning in my core and pinpoint when exactly I had lost my mind and how much longer I would care that I had.

***

As we traveled the next day he allowed me the ability to walk but always stayed well within arm's reach. I don't know that it's because he's scared that I'll run anymore though, and not just because he wants to be close to me. That thought shouldn't have warmth spreading through my chest, and yet.

"What are you going to do with me?" I ask, breaking the silence we've been walking in forever. I've decided firmly I want to know. One can never be too prepared to face their imminent death, though the more time i spend with him the safer im starting to feel.

"Seeing as I stole you, I assumed we were going home," he said, his strides not missing a beat as I stop in my tracks.

"Your home?" I eye his deliciously muscled back as he walks slightly ahead, stopping with a sigh.

"What is it your people are always saying? Finder's keepers?" His grin was bordering on insane and damn did I feel that grin in my toes. He circled back toward me making my heart race slightly. My breath keeping time with his steps.

"That doesn't apply to people," I try to say firmly but my words barely come out a whisper. In a blink he's across the field only a breath away.

"I disagree." His eyes flick down to my lips as his tongue caresses his delicately pointed canines, his silver horns glinting in the sunlight filtering through the trees. I want with every fiber of my being to run my fingers over them, to see if I could feel the masterpiece that looked to be carved into them. Everything about him is absolutely sinful, and boy did I want to rack up a list of transgressions.

I can't move a muscle, and while it doesn't have to do with his blood wielding, it is absolutely because of this hold he has over me. I shouldn't be attracted to my kidnapper. Well rescuer? Second kidnapper? What is he? If he keeps looking down at me like he's going to devour me whole I can't say I'll actually care all that much. Well that certainly didn't take me long to justify, I think to myself grimly.

His head snaps to the side, breaking the spell he has on me and then I hear it too. A river not too far to the west. I would give anything for a bath, but you couldn't pay me to strip in front of him. He seemed to know exactly what I was thinking as he tossed me over his shoulder and broke into a jog toward the rushing water, moving inhumanly fast. I don't know that this is something I'll ever get used to.

"You don't have to pick me up every time you want me to go somewhere specific," I say with a huff, smacking the broad expanse of his back with the flats of my hands.

"You have a history of running when you feel backed into a corner, no? And you need a bath." He made a show of sniffing the air around us and retching. "So, I'm saving myself the trouble of having to catch you." Before he can finish his statement we reach the edge of the babbling river, and he unceremoniously drops me into the water, dunking me in. I resurface sputtering, "you're an ass."

"That is what they call me. Your clothes look a little wet, Dove." He gives that grin that usually takes my knees out. "Remove them."

"Excuse me?" My eyes widen up at him and my entire body flushes pink. There is no way he seriously expects me to take my clothes off with him standing there staring me down.

"Lucky me, I can't trust you not to run, which means I get to watch. Captor's rules." He shrugs, that grin growing to show the indent beside his mouth. The first genuine smile I think I've ever gotten from him, and this is why? Rage blurs my vision as I rip my shirt off, the band covering my breasts barely doing its job after nearly three weeks of traveling with no basic comforts. His eyes are saucers as I bundle my shirt up in a ball, breasts swaying, and then with all the strength I have I hurl my soaked shirt at Asmodeus. It hit him square in the face with a thwack and wrapped around it, effectively tangling him in my mud-covered sweaty shirt. I use the distraction to quickly peel my pants off and toss them to the bank before lowering my entire body out of sight with a satisfied smirk. He got the shirt unwrapped from his head and gave me a look that had me curling my toes into the riverbed.

"Your clothes look a little wet, Ass," I say sweetly, narrowing my eyes at him.

"They do, don't they?" Oh gods, this is backfiring. He hung his thick black cloak over a nearby branch and slowly began unlacing the laces tied loosely at his clavicle before peeling the barely wet shirt from his torso. I greedily watch every centimeter of that shirt come off, taking in his gorgeous body, nearly drooling. I want to make a map of those muscles with my tongue. He crouches along the riverbank collecting my clothes and taking them to a nearby rock to work on cleaning them out. I have to purse my lips to keep my face as close to neutral as possible as I take in his sculpted body.

"I'm not going to hurt you Bryndis," he said tenderly before adding, "not in any way you wouldn't like." The smile that followed didn't quite reach his eyes, though. I know I shouldn't trust him, he's a demon. I shouldn't even like him but there's a part of me that shrivels at him using my name, instead of one of the countless nicknames he's given me.

"You said Lui owes you a favor." I paddle against the slight current to avoid having to get out in nothing more than the flimsy underclothes I'm still wearing, knowing I have no way to distract him while I get out. "Do you have connections in that industry?" I watch him work on the worst of the mud left on the knees of my pants. I say that to justify staring but really, I'm just watching

the way his muscles flex as he moves. Who knew laun-
dry could be so sexy?

"Are you asking me if I'm going to sell you?" He
stopped working, turning his head to meet my eyes warily, looking almost hurt.

"No. I think I know exactly what you plan to do with
me." Chewing on my lower lip, my face flushes; and I
catch myself thinking about all the things awaiting me
when we reach wherever were going and I realize I'm not
repulsed. "I was more wondering if you would be able to
find out who has been taken." Pity lines his eyes as he
looks down at me.

"We don't collect their names officially or anything.
Unless it was someone that would have been highly
marked like you, it's unlikely we would be able to track
them down." He said we? We would track them down.
I'm still trying to adjust to this creature wanting to be
around me, wanting to do more than just be around me.

"What is your end goal, As?"

He studied me for a while before sighing, "It's going
to scare you." He paused weighing his response. "You've
already run so many times, Dove. I couldn't bear it if you
flew away forever."

"Tell me what you want Asmodeus," I say, holding his
eyes from the water.

"Your soul," he said quietly. The longing in his eyes
nearly pulled my heart out of my chest. My throat dried
out. My soul? Like to eat? To keep? What does that even
mean? I thought demons trading in souls was a myth.

"My ultimate goal is to be tied to you forever but whatever you're willing to give me for however long is more than enough. You're all I could have ever asked for, Bryn." He hastily finished his response, like he figured the former would automatically be off limits.

Asmodeus was staring at me waiting for a response, and I was just staring at him open-mouthed, still in the river, quickly turning into a raisin. He just wants me. That's genuinely everything? He really has been straightforward since he rescued me out of that stupid boulder. I'd be lying if I said staying with him sounded unappealing, it's not like there's anywhere else for me to go. It didn't take long for me to make sense of my thoughts and look over at the statuesque man before me trying to find anywhere to look but at me. I moved to the edge of the river, firmly making my decision. This is probably the dumbest thing I'll ever do, but I've never been one to half ass something.

"Asmodeus? I'll make you a deal."

CHAPTER 10

He looked over at me just as I stood from the water, his jaw dropping nearly to the riverbed before he quickly collected himself. I didn't miss the response though, and it gave my ego the boost I desperately needed. Just because the men I knew were immune to my wiles doesn't mean I don't have them; I think to myself firmly.

Drops of river water go racing from my clavicle, dripping down between my breasts, probably not a perfect handful with how big his hands are but I doubt he'd complain. They've all but spilled out of the band around my torso which I'm realizing is see through anyway. I take a deep breath letting the thought pass, determined to make this deal, however I need to. His eyes darkened as I take a step toward him, letting the water run over my toned abdomen and down the long expanse of my legs to reunite with the river. He seems to be tracing every droplet with his eyes. The drops slow, and I realize with a start he's slowing their descent down my body, devouring me like the black hole he is.

"If you help me find my friend and can ensure her continued safety," I cock my head as I pause to make my point. "I'll give you my soul," I take a deep breath, squaring my shoulders, my wet hair clinging to my curves. I will not allow anything else to make me cower. He stands from the clothes he had gingerly laid out to dry and takes a step forward before stopping himself.

"This means you'll be stuck with me until my existence is snuffed out, is that something you're really prepared to offer?" He stares at me questioning but there's something else in his eyes. A deep loneliness, an overwhelming hope.

"If you can promise me she'll be okay, it's yours," I tell him solemnly. It's an easy trade honestly, something splintered and broken for my best friend? He may be getting the bad deal here. I close the distance between us until for once I'm the one putting myself a breath away.

"Do we have a deal?" I whisper, my lips so close to grazing his I can almost feel them and if he pulls away, I might cry. I don't think this is just about making the deal anymore, stupid traitorous vagina.

Looking up at him through my eyelashes, I can see the moment his composure fully breaks. He winds all his long fingers through my hair, yanking back to bring my lips to his in a scorching kiss. Everything about it is consuming. My wet body molding to his, the drops of water turning to steam. His skin is almost too hot, nearly burning me as he kisses me senseless. He shifts one hand from the back of my skull to the base of my throat completely wrapping around my neck.

When his tongue parts my lips my skin ignites, a sweet burn concentrating on my left forearm. I run my fingers through the silky stands of his hair, using it to draw him closer. He trails his hands down my nearly naked body stopping on my ass to lift me up, giving it an appreciative squeeze as I wrap my legs around his torso, clinging to him with everything in me. The burning on my arm intensifies and then all at once it's gone and all that's left is the feel of his soft lips, his warm skin on mine, his teeth nipping at my bottom lip; and then the trail of kisses he traces from my lips back to my ear where he whispers, "it's a deal."

CHAPTER 11

I spend the next hour describing every possible thing about Libby that comes to mind as my clothes dry, wearing the shirt he so generously gave me after setting me down gently. My face flushed the second my feet hit the ground and I found myself unable to look up at into his abyssal eyes until I was dressed again. He seems confident enough in his abilities to track her down but there is kind of a lot riding on his ability to do so. He questions multiple times that she's a human, which I assume is due to her size. The mental image of her has my stomach twisting. It's been weeks since we lost each other and there's a part of me that worries she won't want to see me.

Asmodeus starts working on setting up camp, still well in eye shot and I see his black eyes regularly turning to land on me. Almost as if he feared I would just vanish, nothing but a dream. The idea that a being would jump at the opportunity to be shackled to me until they were dust feels impossible; and yet there's a brand banded around my left arm with the intricate spirals on his horns woven into it, an official indicator of our bargain. The burn during our kiss. It'll become a permanent connection to him should he succeed to fulfill his end of our deal, at least that's what he told me, noting my shock upon seeing the brand before I pulled his shirt on.

He allowed me space to dress in my own clothes, and when I got back to our little camp he had moved back to the riverbank and was braiding together a chain of daisies. The little flowers just starting to grow again as the bogs transformed into woodlands.

"What are you doing?" I questioned, seeing the tiny flowers in his weirdly large hands was almost comical.

"I'm making you a crown, so you have a piece of your friend until we find her." My heart melts. I sit beside him watching him finish the last of the braid.

"How do you know how to do that?"

"I have existed longer than I care to remember. A braid is no feat, Bryndis." He scoffs and shakes his head before he stills, poking his tongue out of the corner of his perfect mouth while he focuses on tying off the circlet and puts it onto my head.

"Thank you, Asmodeus." I genuinely mean it, my eyes well up with tears feeling the crown on my head again. He is the first living creature outside of Libby that has shown me genuine unwavering kindness in my life. I lean over and brush a kiss onto his cheek. I didn't know demons could blush, but his cheeks turn bright pink for just a flash before he wields his blood back in line.

I can feel the energy buzzing through my brand as he wields his power, causing me to gasp. "I felt that."

"I would hope so, it's a direct line to me, Dove. The only time you won't feel it anymore is if I'm dead." The concept causes my heart to sink. Not the fact that it's a direct line, the idea that he could die. I shut the thought down as fast as I can. This is a business interaction, Bryn. I mentally scold myself. We can look but no more touching, not if this will be the reaction. I think about how soft his cheek was under my lips, even with the stubble that was starting to cross the border into a beard and how it felt to run my fingers through that mane of hair. Well, maybe a little touching. My brain is ping ponging between not even looking at him anymore and climbing him like one of the trees surrounding us.

"Do you have any questions? I'll admit I've never made it this far into accumulating a soul and I only know how it's supposed to work in theory." He looks over at me, realizing I've stayed silent for quite a while as my thoughts spin, entirely on trying to justify how I can allow such an unhealthy attraction.

"You've never taken another soul?" My thoughts stop.

"No. I've had my fair share of women, demon and human, but never one with a soul I've wanted. Not one I would want forever. That's kind of a one-time deal." He said slowly, gauging my reaction. Seemingly very confused.

Well, you did just hyper fixate on the fact that he's been single instead of the potential eternity bound to him, so the confusion makes sense, doesn't it? I mentally scold myself and realize we've fallen into silence again. How long has he been wandering around and I'm who he wants forever? I let a single smothered butterfly loose, enjoying his desire for every aspect of me.

Since the brand he's been much more distant. Physically anyway, like he doesn't always feel the need to be breathing my air and I hate myself for it but I kind of miss being encompassed by him. We're still not sitting far apart by any means, but I peek over at him slyly. He's doing everything he can not to look in my direction, the sound of the bugs around us deafening in the silence. If I slowly start shifting, I bet I could make it over to him without him noticing. I have to keep myself from chuckling at this stupid little game I've just made for myself. I can feel him through the brand, let's see how well. Slowly, I start to scoot across the dirt. Inching painfully slow. The slightest twinge and I stop, looking innocently everywhere but Asmodeus.

I do this until I'm nearly brushing his side. The moment I'm close enough he grabs me with lightning speed and spins me into his lap. I can't stop the frantic giggle that burbles past my lips. He's securely folded me into him, using his lap and arms as a cradle. The amusement glittering in his depthless eyes making that single butterfly turn into a swarm.

"I can feel you too, you're not sneaky little Dove." He grins down at me, booping my nose gently. My giggles abruptly stop, my thoughts sobering me up quickly. Looking up at his sparkling face I really can't understand.

"Why me?" My voice comes out so small that I want to smack myself.

"The second you looked me dead in the eyes and gave me the finger like you knew my history, I was a goner." He grins down at me, and I playfully swat at his chest, shaking my head. I move to stand, but he holds me firmly in his lap.

"I'm not joking, Bryndis," he continued. "I have spent a long time waiting for my equal. Seeing your rage that day, That surety of yourself even in an impossible situation." He shook his head momentarily at a loss for words. His eyes swirled, an entire cosmos completely dedicated to me.

"I've never seen something so fierce. I couldn't look away, not even just then but for days. I wanted to bask in every bit of destruction you would render and appreciate it for the masterpiece it was. You are a force Bryn, and I want to follow in your wake as you burn this world to ash." His eyes twinkle down at me, cupping my face in his large hand.

I should not be feeling this, but he's shown himself to be nothing but good. Well neutral. Maybe a little chaotic, but doesn't everything deserve love? No one has ever had anything nice to say about me, and yet here this creature is, loving even the parts of me I thought should be hated. I reach up and cup his face in my palm in return, he relaxes into it like all he could ever want is my touch. I trace the line of his lips with my thumb, and looking up at him I think for once we're on the same page. Taking the daisy crown off my head, I plop it onto his giggling to myself.

"Does this make me king for tonight?" He asked eyes darkening and I shivered in his hold. Hand still adjusting his little crown, I take the opportunity that has finally presented itself and slowly run my index finger along the spiraling length of one of his horns. They're completely smooth as bone outside of the ridges every few inches. I feel his entire body shudder before he grabs my wrist. "I think that's enough trouble for you today, my little anarchist." He stands bringing me with him to set me down on my feet. "Can I trust you not to go anywhere while I find something to eat?" I nod, begrudging of him leaving me.

I sit down by the fire fully prepared to give him an earful when he returns about how much of an anarchist I can be, but the warmth wraps me up and I fall into a fitful sleep.

***

We begin our travels back the way we came bright and early. Asmodeus didn't seem to mind that we were going in circles, just seemed to thoroughly enjoy every second of our jaunt through the woods together. Since he scooped me up out of that boulder, I feel safe, loved, happy even. Emotions I didn't realize I could feel. Things are so easy, just like they were with Libby. I feel like I fit with him. There's something much different here though, every boundary I've ever made for myself is slowly being pushed. Peering up at his back shifting under his black shirt and remembering his fingers clasped around the column of my throat have those lines blurring quicker and quicker. There's never been an instance when someone has been able to make me feel this secure. This relationship is unlike anything I could have anticipated; but that's not really what it is, is it? This is ownership.

Am I actually upset about that though? If I'm going to belong to anyone, I could do much worse than the embodiment of starlight before me. Is it ownership when he's given me every opportunity to be his equal when he's able? I've never felt like this, never been treated like this before, and I don't know what to do with my swirling emotions. It's hard to remember what got us to this point when all I can think about is running my hands through his glossy black hair and seeing what kind of reaction fully grabbing his horns would get me. I'm practically drooling over him, following him blindly into the bog; every shred of my sanity completely gone, but this is the least crazy I've ever felt.

Right when I'm about to really lay into myself mentally he turns with a smile that has my mind emptying out completely. He looks so happy, the dark shadows under his eyes lightened, his smiles freely illuminating his entire face now. My heart gives a painful squeeze, I have no complaints about this situation.

"I get to carry you now," he states matter of factly, his brilliant smile stealing my breath. "Lest I lose you to the mud again." He winks and I smile, shaking my head as I walk toward him to wrap my arms around his shoulders allowing him to smoothly lift me. We've gotten very good at that; I think to myself as he starts walking.

It's been a while since we've been like this, this time I can't seem to look away from his face. The butterflies in my stomach have turned into bats and I can't help mooning over him as he carries me along like a gallant knight. My knight. He notices almost immediately and gives me a grin that stops my heart. When he breaks our eye contact to pay attention to the trail it feels like a loss, it's then that it hits me.

I think I'm in love with him. I've fallen in love with a demon.

CHAPTER 12

We've been walking through the bog for most of the day, moving much faster now that he's carrying me. My head is rested into the crook of his neck, dozing. I have never been this comfortable anywhere.

"I don't think I've been carried like this since I was a baby." I yawn, straightening a little in a subtle request to stretch my legs. He gently set me down.

"Really?" He questioned, appraising me head to toe.

"I mean my mom died during The Rise and my dad was imprisoned not long after so, yeah." I shrug as he looks at me questioningly. "What?" I laugh at his bewildered expression.

"Well, a lot of things, first that I'm sorry." I shrug again, but he looks me in the eyes, running a fingertip along the underside of my chin. "Something so precious should always be treated as such and I hate that you weren't." His eyes are boring holes into me. "I've also never heard of a human referring to this as The Rise." He smiled gesturing around himself. "I knew I picked well." He grinned at me waiting for an answer to his non question.

"Yeah, well you have my father to thank for that." I walk away from him, the memory of him too painful to dwell on. Idly, I pick at leaves on the trail, trying to keep my mind steady, so I could fully explain. "He was a bit of an activist, I suppose. He refused to believe demons were inherently evil, regardless of what had happened with my mother. He was a good man, just a little crazy. He genuinely believed the world was better with you all in it, and he actively fought against any form of government the people around us tried to establish. It was his downfall. I can't remember his face, but I'll never forget the way he saw the world." My heart gave a good squeeze at the memory of him.

"And what do you believe?" Asmodeus asked standing beside me. I finally look up, turning my face to meet his eyes.

"I believe that Monsters were here long before the rift." He's nodding in appreciation of my answer. I turn to face him fully, allowing myself to let the walls I so carefully built down. He opens his mouth to say something.

Crashing coming through the trees to my left was the only precursor to the pain as something barreled into my side, knocking me completely across the path into a tree on the opposite side of the trail. I slumped against it, trying to catch the air that had been thoroughly flung from me. I frantically start looking for Asmodeus, making sure he hadn't also been pummeled.

Nothing could have prepared me for the sight of my knight, hanging from the tree near where I had just been standing, a thick branch all the way through his abdomen skewering him. My jaw dropped open, but he just smiled down at me.

"It's just a scratch darling." He was pulling himself off the branch slowly. I didn't have time to process the gruesome scene before a demon, much like Lui, grabbed me by the throat. His deep green hand too big to properly fit in the space, making me crane my neck back toward the sky, cutting off the flow of oxygen into my lungs. I will not die like this. Viciously I start clawing at the hand, letting rage drive every movement. The demon lifted me and as my toes left the ground, cutting off what little air I had left. Terrified, I resorted to kicking and thrashing but nothing was breaking his hold on me.

I glance across the field to Asmodeus still stuck on the branch, my vision going spotty, but he gives me a nod as his powers erupt through me from the brand. I can feel every atom of water surrounding me. The beads in the dirt, the molecules in the air. The strong flow of blood through the six demons that attacked us. I smile as I take hold of the giant holding me, forcing his entire hand open to release me. I plop to the ground, landing on my feet, adrenaline soaring. Focusing my will on moving his legs, I sloppily force the eight-foot demon to cross the trail and grab one of his own gang; a beady eyed demon on a leash, one Professor Sanford had taught us about. I make the green demon rip its pet in half, acids from the sacks around its midsection raining down on the giant and three of the other demons around it, their skin boiling off, their bones melting into the muddy ground. Just like that four of six died in a cacophony of screams and shrieks. I took hold of the other two demons' bodies, forcing them to face me. They looked like Asmodeus' kind, both bright red with wide black eyes finally understanding the gravity of the situation they've put themselves in.

My knight in shining armor has removed himself from the tree, dropping to the ground and was brushing his shirt off as his abdomen healed. He came to check on me first, looking me over before leaning forward.

"Good girl," he whispered in my ear as I forced the demons left standing to kneel, allowing Asmodeus his revenge for being impaled. He removes a curved knife from his boot, as he walks toward the still kneeling demons. I see firsthand why no one put serious effort into catching him when he stole me. Their deaths were not swift by any means, and I can do nothing but sit back and revel at his wrath. He finished flaying the demons and I let their muscles finally loosen to slump to the ground next to their partners. The brand on my arm tingled as the power he lent me dissipated.

"You're welcome." He says over his shoulder as he stands cleaning his knife off before stowing it back in his boot. Spinning slowly, he looks back at me like he could eat me alive; he runs his tongue over his lower lip as he stalks toward me, making me shudder under his gaze. He just gave me his power, handed it over without a second thought, so I could save myself in a situation I never would have prevailed in. This was absolutely more than ownership. I take a step toward the being I'm now bound to, fully intending to show how him exactly how thankful I am. Whether we find Libby or not he's stuck with me, especially after this. The fear of seeing him impaled making my feelings for him crystal clear.

I would follow that man to the ends of every world in the galaxy of his black eyes. The mighty beating of wings sounding not far in the distance had our heads turning before I could reach his side. Within a moment, Lui lands with a solid thud on the trail littered with corpses.

"Looks like ya got yerslef in a bit of a pickle there, Ass." He smiled down at Asmodeus.

No, His nickname wasn't actually ass, there's no way that's a term of endearment to them. Yet there he was, striding toward Lui, grinning ear to ear, to clasp his giant hand in his in greeting. I didn't realize they were friends.

"Hello again Lui." I approach cautiously. He did steal me from the woods after all.

"Oi if it isn't the hellhound 'erself." He raised his hands up in mock praise. "Glad he got you out of there without too much trouble. It's not every day we get one like you roaming around these parts and Ass has needed someone to kick him into shape for a while." He winked at me with those golden eyes. He planned this and given the sheer shock on Asmodeus' face; he clearly was made to think it was his own idea.

"Were you the one that left her door open?" Asmodeus asked in shock. The door to my little pod was just sitting open?

"Only someone who can wield the earth can do that, you know I need to enlist em every time we get in a new rescue." He shrugs at us both. I'm thoroughly confused. Rescues? Then it all clicks into place.

They're working within a trafficking ring to save the girls they find alone wandering through the woods before anyone else can get to them. Lui grabbed me to help me, but instead decided to bait As into being the hero in the story, giving us both exactly what we needed.

I left to give them some time together to catch up and went foraging for some berries to kill the time, I have been getting much better at bog hopping and avoiding the worst of the muds that can suck you right under. By the time I got back they had migrated a bit closer to the demon market and had posted themselves up on the trail waiting for me.

"I got some news for ya doll." Lui smirked at me from where he was sitting as I cleared the trees. Asmodeus looked at me grinning ear to ear as he said, "I think I know where we can find Libby."

| 83 |

CHAPTER 13

Lui took off as soon as we started moving, heading toward my best friend. Asmodeus carried me the rest of the way to the demon market, and it wasn't long after the sun set that we were strolling through the gates. Neither of us has had a decent night sleep since we met, and I think it's starting to wear on us both. My eyes are bleary as he leads me into the market, to a grouping of buildings in the center, the path between them lit by torches. He doesn't take long talking to an inconsequential burnt orange demon with fin like ears in a language I couldn't dream of speaking. Listening to them closer I realized their tongues were split, that's how they were capable of saying those unheard-of consonants.

Upon receiving a tiny bronze key from the minuscule creature, he led me through the small buildings off to the side until we stop in front of the furthest door at the end attached to a structure that's no more than a hut. He gives me a half bow, gesturing me through the door frame as it swung open.

Of course, the room is as small as physically possible with a bed taking up almost the entire room in the middle. It looked to be able to fit a demon as big as Lui if necessary. I look over at Asmodeus, face only illuminated by the single lantern he was carrying. The fire raged in his black eyes, bringing them to life. He really is far too beautiful for his own good. I move into the room toward the bed taking in the furs and hand sewn blankets covering it.

"I hope you don't mind sharing, Dove. There's no such thing as a multiple bed room in this kind of market." He smiled anxiously at me, as if he didn't just give me the greatest gift anyone has ever given me, the ability to save myself without a second thought. I don't say anything to him, just turn from the bed to face him in the doorway. His eyes widen as I slowly walk toward him, coming right up to his face, his chin in line with my nose. I reach behind him and shut the door, never breaking eye contact with him.

"You didn't mind sharing back there, with your power I mean." I clear my throat suddenly getting very nervous. "I didn't know we could do that." I glance at his lips starting to lose my nerve, I've never even been alone with a man, let alone someone that looks like an angel stuck in a human body. I don't really know how to go about initiating this.

"I didn't either, I knew being bound to each other had to mean something, until you give me what's mine." His eyes narrowed in a way I wouldn't have understood even a week ago. "It turns out it's for your protection. I just had to think about you using my power and then you were."

"You have that much faith in me? Who's to say that green demon wouldn't have snapped my neck? Or that I wouldn't have used your power against you?" I try to goad him into breaking some of the composure he's so carefully maintained since the kiss.

"You aren't a woman that needs saving. You are much more capable than I was in that moment." He looked down at me, his black eyes glinting dangerously. "I've never encountered a human I've wanted like is. Lui spoke of putting me in my place and I've realized exactly where that is. My place is at your feet, worshiping you like the goddess you are. I am nothing more than a tool meant to be wielded by you. A flame for you to ignite this world. Take my heart, take my soul, take my power, its all yours." He brushed the strands of hair back from my face. "You are my salvation, and you will be my doom," he whispers, bringing his lips down on mine for the first time since the day we made our bargain.

He kisses me like there has never been and will never be anyone else. So tenderly my eyes start to fill with tears, it's easy to shove them back down as the lantern clatters to the floor, quickly plunging us into blackness. There is nothing but the feel of his lips on mine, his hands gingerly holding my face for him to have full access to me. I gasp as the backs of my legs bump into the bed frame, and we topple over onto the bed in a tangle in limbs. He uses that gasp to his advantage and runs his silky tongue along my lower lip, tasting me. He groans pulling back to trail kisses along my chin.

"Perfection," he murmurs skimming his lips down the column of my throat. The feather-light touch is driving me crazy. Reaching up to put my hands on his chest, I start untying the laces to this shirt when I lose the capability to move my hands. I freeze, his laughter skates my collar bones.

"So impatient, Dove." He nips at the base of my neck causing me to shudder. His sharp canines scratching my skin, the pain something I would beg for.

"I want to give you a gift. To repay you." I don't want to beg to go down on him but I'm about two seconds from it when he steals my breath.

"Why would you ever think this," he pauses, running a hand from my hip all the way up my body to the side of my face. "Isn't my gift?" He wraps his hand around my throat, and I arch up into his hold, submitting to him completely.

He growls as our lips meet again, this time claiming me in every way. Our tongues collide, exploring each other, and he finally gives me my hands back. He tugs the laces of my vest open and quickly sets to work removing my shirt and everything under it in one swift movement. His hands coming back to stroke my shoulders in tantalizing strokes slowly working his way down my arms and back up, making a trail to my chest. Two can play that game. I start gently running my fingertips under the seam of his shirt to trace the lines of his abdominal muscles, he shudders.

"Stop that," he said, voice hoarse.

"Then take your shirt off," I quip back at him, nipping at his bottom lip. His weight is off me briefly and when its back it's the direct warmth of his overheated skin. I feel his chest, finally placing both hands firmly on the silky skin of pecs but I can't help the involuntary pucker of my bottom lip. He runs a finger along it.

"What's wrong, My Dove?" He asks, immediately softening, pulling away to look more closely at my face. I didn't realize he could see in the dark that well.

"I just want to see you," I say feeling slightly stupid.

His laughter coats my skin as he presses a gentle kiss to my pursed lip. "And greedy?" He says lifting himself from the bed to relight the lantern. "How did I get this lucky?" His honeyed voice rumbled through the darkness before the room was cast in shadow. He hung the lantern on the hook beside the door and it was the perfect amount of light to see his chiseled features. The shadows of his horns curving menacingly in front of me making my thighs clench together. Noting the movement, his mouth ticked up.

He tskd at me as he slowly prowled back toward the bed, hunting me, if that's even possible in five feet of space. I went to scooch further into the massive mattress, but he wrapped his fingers around my ankles pulling me back to him, standing at the edge of the bed.

"What about my gift, Bryndis?" His teeth glint in the fire light as he lifts to open my legs in a perfect 'v' in front of him. My heart sputters, there isn't a thought in my brain as he slowly runs his fingers up the entire length of my legs from the sides of my feet before meeting at my belt. He paused, looking down at me questioningly. Giving me a chance to change my mind before this goes any farther. Meeting his eyes I nod vigorously, incapable of speech, and within seconds he has my pants flying across the room to rest in the corner.

He roughly tugs me by my hips partially off the mattress and kneels, looking up at me. I squirm in his hold. "Are you going sit still or am I going to have to make you?" He questioned nipping at my inner thigh, I yelped shifting myself exactly back to where he had me in response. "That's my girl." He licked over the spot he just bit into, soothing the ache, leaving an entirely different kind of pain. He grabs the waistline of my panties and rips them off as if they were made of paper.

Now completely bare before him. He starts a maddening ascent of leisurely kisses along my inner thigh, running his tongue along my skin tauntingly. I can't hold back my moan as his breath fans across my overheated skin. If he doesn't move faster, I might combust. I grab one of his horns in an effort to steer him, and he jerks, his eyes sucking up the firelight as he looks up at me.

"Naughty girl." He stands, moving up to hover over my body. I'm so distracted by lust I haven't even realized I've lost control of my muscles, I don't even care. He positions my hands above my head, offering my breasts up to him. Licking his lips looking down at my naked flesh, he circles the bed. "What to do with you?" He purrs tapping his pursed lips.

"I've got a couple ideas," I bite at him frustrated by the precarious position I've found myself In.

"I'm sure you do, Dove." He croons down at me and stops before reaching down to run a single finger along the inseam of my foot.

I can't squirm and the sensation borders on painful. I fight with my now locked lips to try to tell him to stop as he moves further up my body to tickle my armpits still completely exposed. "Oh, don't we like this?" He only releases the hold on my lips, every other muscle firmly frozen. "I'll give you what you want, but only if you ask nicely." He leans forward to run his tongue quickly across one of my nipples, causing it to peak at the sudden cold as he moves away. He bites and kisses a trail along my sternum all the way back down to my thighs where he stops, staring up at me. Those black eyes watching me, waiting.

"Please," I whine, and that bastard had the audacity to chuckle at me. He really could just sit there all night.

"Not good enough." His breath gives me goosebumps as it caresses my tender sex.

"As, please I'm begging you. I need you." The sound barely leaving my mouth.

"I told you this time wouldn't be sarcastic." He doesn't even give me a second to breathe before he dives face first into my pussy, eating me like I was the last meal he'd ever have. Speaking that ethereal language straight to my core.

If I could have arched off the bed, I would have but my muscles remain firmly locked, nothing but a choked whimper escaping my lips. The wave is building and I'm riding it like I wish I could be riding his face. My orgasm reaches its crescendo, hurling me straight to hell with my cruel knight and I revel in the burn.

I'm panting, slowly coming back to reality; still in the bed in the middle of the demon market, Asmodeus resting his cheek on my thigh. I lift my head, realizing my muscles were free again, and reached down to run my fingers through his tousled hair. "If you had been a good girl we would have kept going, but I think that's enough for tonight." He grins kissing the bite mark he left on my thigh as he shifts up to lay beside me curling him into my body. Kept going? My head is still swimming in a cocktail of endorphins, and I couldn't find it in me to do anything but curl up into his warmth and fall into the deepest sleep of my life.

CHAPTER 14

My eyes don't blink open until the sun is about halfway in the sky. As is still next to me, my limbs wrapped around his. I'm naked. The realization acts like an ice bath. I start and sit abruptly to grab the blankets, looking for my clothes. Asmodeus stretches next to me, disturbed by the sudden cold. His muscles flexing as his back popped. Lazily he opened his eyes to grin at me, half asleep.

"Where are we going?" He asked groggily as I stood, taking all the blankets with me.

"I am finding my clothes." I scrunch my eyebrows at him, but I can't find it in me to a put effort into scowling at the sleepy demon.

"Why ever would you do such a thing?" He grabbed his chest aghast, opening his eyes all the way before moving at that inhuman speed to grab the edge of the blankets trailing behind me from the bed. He gives them a firm tug and they slip to my breast line. I yelp and accumulate all my blankets back up to my chin. He smiles savagely, pulling the bundle harder, bringing me shooting back the three paces to the bed to land neatly into his arms. Bundled onto his chest, my face only inches from his, that smile softens.

"You don't have to be shy, My Dove," he says as he kisses the tip of my nose, "stay with me for a minute." He settled into the bed with me on top of him, my elbows propping me up on his chest.

"You seemed so confident you knew where my friend was and yet you're stalling." I grimace down at the sleeping angel I'm perched on. He cracks a black eye open.

"I do." He starts very slowly, drawing out each syllable. "There are just some things we need to talk about first." His expression sobers, both eyes locked onto mine. "Lui had some very interesting information that confirmed what I had been suspecting." I stare at him, waiting for him to finish. "I'm pretty confident she's still in this town, we just need to find her." I just keep staring at him, my brain a jumble of questions, unsure which to ask first. The only one without follow ups seems like a good place to start.

"Town? I thought this was a market." I think back on the few stalls I caught a glimpse of but couldn't place what they would have been selling, I didn't get a good enough look.

"The entrance is a market, whoever comes in the kingdom has to see all the wares up for offer and pass over them to get to their destination. Its diabolical when you think of it." He chuckles to himself over demon economics.

I shake my head at him, so further in people live here? Do they have a government and agricultural systems and everything? He said kingdom. I'm so confused. I knew my knowledge was limited but I didn't realize how nearly human they were. Turns out I have a lot of follow up questions, but none of them are as important as the topic of my friend.

"And you think Libby is just living here?" I ask trying to organize my thoughts again. He sighs below me and shifts to sit us both up on the bed. He sits me down across from him to put some space between us. Still shirtless, in the light I can fully see the swirling bands of ink along his left arm and up his chest, nearly matching Lui's just smaller. Yet another question.

"Bryndis, did you know Libby's parents?" He asked me, his blank stare a mask for his swirling thoughts, as if he couldn't find the words to say what he needed to.

"I mean I knew her mom vaguely, she was a very interesting woman. I'm pretty sure she's where Libby's love of trinkets came from." I smile to myself, remembering the shelves lined with tiny things hung from the beams of her yurt.

"Yeah, that would make sense. We're pretty sure Libby's father was one of us." He just said it. Dropped a bomb right in my face. I sit there, jaw on the floor waiting for him to elaborate. There's no way my tiny curly haired friend was half demon, was there?

"I don't know what happened to her Bryn, her story is her own." He sighs looking so torn. "I had seen a girl mostly matching your description of Libby running around the market, but she's an imp. She has the horns and the wings…"

"And the tail." I finish for him finally fully meeting his eyes. "So, you've seen her?" I finish trying to process what I'm hearing, and he nods gravely. "How?"

"Our traits can remain dormant until there's a need for them, like a biological defense meant to keep our spawn hidden. Our mating with humans is possible but wasn't intended, there's still much we don't know. More often than not humans are branded before they have children. My best guess is that when she was taken the adrenaline rushing her system was all she needed to make the shift." I just stare at him. Blinking.

Libby had never even been looked at all that weird because of my constant vicious defense of her. Outside of her mother's passing I can't think of anything else in her life that would have caused that much stress. Her trinkets were weirdly spread around the trail because she was flying.

"So Lui has seen her? He confirmed this?" The fact that she's really within the same gates as me causes a bubble of joy to well up in my chest that fill my eyes with tears.

"Yeah, he's been taking great care of her," he mumbled, a glint in his eyes like there's a lot to that story I may not want to know. He reaches out and wipes the tears now freely flowing down my face. "I know it's a lot to take in, she's still your friend though Bryn, just a little different."

I stiffened, sniffling. He thinks I'm crying because of who she is? I'm currently essentially the ward of a demon with no complaints. Hell I'd recommend it, if we take last night into account.

"I'm not crying because I'm sad, Ass." I smile over at him, and I ruffle his hair. The face that had been a mask of indifference breaking to show sheer relief. "You told me with confidence that you've seen her, and she's alive. The details don't matter." I move onto my knees letting the blankets slip down around my waist as I crawl into his lap. Looking down at him I pull a fistful of his hair back to look up at me.

"I happen to be getting very used to demons." I graze my lips lightly along his.

"Oh? Just getting used to us?" He quips back but his breath hitches. I'll never get used to the idea that he wants me just as badly as I want him.

"I could certainly be persuaded into a firm like." I kiss his lips firmly before rising from the bed. The sun is starting to set and the market outside was beginning to bustle. "Now come on, we have places to be and people to find."

It's time to track down my best friend.

CHAPTER 15

I quickly dressed as Asmodeus locates his shirt, forego-ing the cloak now that we're back on a mostly noctur-nal schedule.

"Here's how this is going to work." He turned toward me menacingly, making my stomach drop to my toes in excitement. "We're going to go through this market to look for Libby, but we are going to take our time and set up deliveries to my home for anything you may need once we leave here. Once I get you home all to myself you won't be leaving for a while." He tossed me a wink, and I caught exactly what he was saying. My entire chest flushed as he continued. "You will not run, you will not leave my side, you will not give me any sass for however I choose to spoil you." I sat there ticking things off on my fingers earning a glare from him. "If you see anything you like, say the word and it's yours."

He wrapped an arm around my waist herding me out the door of the tiny hut and into the market. There was too much to take in and I was immediately overwhelmed. The stalls were practically overlapping each other, each selling everything anyone could possibly need. Foods, books, furniture, jewelry. There was even a stall I could see promoting cursed objects. What could I possibly need here? Almost everything was geared to the demons filtering through the walkways.

Asmodeus moved leisurely from stall to stall, knowing exactly what he was looking for and where to find them. He was buying so many things it was making my head spin. I knew he was not someone to be trifled with, but by the way that these demons are prostrating themselves before him, you'd think he's a god. He doesn't have to do much more than point in the direction of what he wants, and the shop owner is tripping over themselves to make it so.

Our first elongated stop was in the stall of a woodworker he clearly knew well. The small creature was as black as night and only came up to my knee, slithering among the shadows of his stall, the only sign he was still there the green eyes that almost seemed to glow. Asmodeus ordered us a new bed, insisting we need one as big as the one in the hut. I let my mind drift on that as he shows me a menagerie of sketches of different chairs and bed frames and everything in between. Outside of basic requests I leave the details to him. He got more plates and cutlery and chairs for around his home, so I have a place to sit in every room. It seems a bit excessive but he's so happy picking all this new furniture that I just nod along with everything he enthusiastically shows me. He sits designing each piece with the small demon and I sit studying his face until he's satisfied and leading me out of the stall, smiling contently.

The next little tent we duck into is what looks like a seamstress's shop. the weathered canvas walls lined with bolts of every fabric imaginable, in every possible color. As picks out at least a hundred fabrics in various colors and sends me to the back with a half imp like Libby. The extremely kind, soft spoken older woman took her time measuring me and we discussed my preferences in how dresses, shirts and pants should fit and move. The idea of a completely custom wardrobe I didn't have to sew myself has my head spinning. She ushers me to a corner of the back absolutely loaded down with lacey undergarments once we finish. I flush, realizing I did, very much need them; Asmodeus tearing my only pair in half had me walking around very exposed today.

"We'll take one of each, thank you," Asmodeus said from behind me, turning my face scarlet. The stout woman merely nodded at him and started accumulating the embarrassing amount of fabric.

"This is kind of a lot As." I lose function of my lips

"I will spoil you however I see fit," he says simply. "And if you keep being so good I may have an extra treat for you." He licks his perfect lips and my core heats.

We have been at this for hours and the night is starting to give way to dawn, as we leave the seamstress. We head back toward our rented hut. As we walk Asmodeus notices a small armory tucked into a corner. He pulls me in, grinning like a mad man. The canvas walls are covered by sheets of wood.

"See anything you like?" He asks gesturing to a wall of weaponry hung up for patrons to view and try.

"This is too much Asmodeus; I have my dagger and some throwing knives. Please, you've already gotten everything I could possibly need." He gives me a look, his lips thinning as he grabs a new set of throwing knives and a short sword, handing it to the demon that had almost magically popped up next to him, refusing to even look him in the eye.

"I'm going to teach you how to use that." He gestures to the sword, his eyes glint with wicked amusement at what I assume is the thought of me drilling with it. I just shake my head at him letting him steer me out to pick up a few more random things, one of them being dye so I can touch up the red in my hair that's mostly faded now. We walk slowly back, and he wraps his arm around me, pulling me close to him. The sun is well in the sky when we reach the entrance of the hut community.

"If she's here she'll be packing up by now, we'll find her tomorrow when we cover the other half." He presses a kiss to my temple as we walk, trying to reassure me. The idea of another full day of this man shopping for me has my stomach twisting a little bit.

I haven't been as in a rush to find her, not now that I know she's safe, especially not if what As had alluded to about her and Lui was true. I don't know how to connect the dots between my kidnapper and my best friend's potential lover. It's hard enough trying to swallow the fact that I wasn't in any real danger. I try to clear my head as we walk through our door. He's spent the entire day doing everything in his power to ensure my comfort, I don't want him to think my silent processing is because of him. I giggle up at him when he picks me up and chucks me through the air onto the bed, my landing scooting it, bumping into the wall.

"I doubt the owner will be too happy with holes in their walls." I grin at him.

"I'd pay to see that urchin work up the nerve to say something about it." He stalks toward the bed. "I've had to walk around with you all day knowing the clothes I can see are the only ones on you." My face flushes, not realizing he had noticed. I want to do something for him though. I've never even seen him without his pants on, which really doesn't seem fair.

"Do you trust me, As?" I shyly look up at his towering form, and he almost shrinks into himself at the question.

"Of course, Dove."

"Enough to strip and give me your power?" I don't know how else to ask without just doing it.

Without another word he quickly ripped his shirt off and started working on his belt. I can feel the swirling of his power start funneling through the brand, slowly heightening my senses until it's like that day in the forest. I could count the water droplets around us again but without the adrenalin I'm completely overwhelmed. How he lives like this all the time is beyond me, I would never be able to focus. His hands stopped unbuckling his pants, his entire body freezing. He looked at me questioningly and I realized I had no idea what I was doing, just reaching out blindly for the water around us. I didn't know how to move the individual muscles just whole pieces and I definitely didn't know how to back off once I had something under thrall. He siphoned his power back a little, so I still had a hold on him but one he could fight if necessary.

"We'll work on that." He promised, struggling to get his zipper down with his locked arms.

"I appreciate the effort love, but it's okay." I chuckle at him, kneeling to be able to wrap my hands around the back of his neck. "You can take it back, I don't think I'll use it after all." His eyes had widened, and he stopped struggling. We stared at each other in complete silence, and he made no move to take the power back.

"As?" I question, starting to worry he's having some sort of stroke or that I've somehow completely frozen up his body again. I wave my hand in front of his face trying to break the daze he seemed to be in. His power drains out through the brand in a whoosh.

"Did you just..." he started shaking his head.

"What?" I laugh.

"You just called me love. Bryndis, do you love me?" His face was blank. Surely, I couldn't have said that. My laughter abruptly stops, my eyes widening at the realization that I did, in fact, say that and heat burns my face. I drop my hands from his neck and sit back down on the bed, my heart starting to pound.

"You call me love all the time Asmo- "

"You have never once said that to me before Bryndis, do not lie to me." He growls at me from where he stands. The rage of being denied his answer bubbling under the surface of his composed facade, his tense jaw the only thing giving him away.

He's barely holding it together and I don't know why. I don't know what I'm supposed to say here, what answer he's looking for. I don't know if the truth is going to send him out the door to never be seen again. He was after my soul, after companionship. This is very different. Even though he calls me love regularly we've never discussed exactly what this relationship is and where our boundaries are because being totally honest, I didn't have any. I just stare at him open-mouthed. If he left so close to me getting the happily ever after I never thought I would get, I don't know how I'll recover. I want to vomit; tears burning the back of my eyes. The idea of him rejecting me tearing my guts out of my body and leaving them mangled at his feet.

"Bryn, answer me." I cover my face with my hands trying to breathe back the tears, trying to figure out how to rewind five minutes. He softens moving to sit on the edge of the bed and grabs my hands pulling them from my face.

"Fuck, just say something," he pleads, and I realized we've been sitting here in silence for what feels like a thousand years.

"I don't know what to say." I look at him worried, and he looks back at me confused.

"I mean you could just say the truth." He shrugs, but the movement is anything but casual. I stare at him, taking in every feature, memorizing every detail in preparation for him to be disgusted. I don't know that anything that has happened hasn't just been a game to win my soul and that I haven't fallen for it so thoroughly that I fell in love with yet another monster. I take a deep breath and when I open my mouth to speak all that comes out is "yes."

"Yes, what?" He growls grabbing my shoulders and shaking slightly out of frustration.

"Yes, I love you." Nothing but a blank stare. I close my eyes not able to look into that beautiful face, I can't stop the words that keep tumbling from my mouth. "I know that this isn't what you were after, and I understand if I've maybe read into things. Love and sex don't have to go hand in hand and if you don't feel the same this doesn't have to change the bargain we can- " he cuts me off with a firm kiss. My mind empties.

When he pulls back, I can see the water glistening in the corner of his eyes. This demon, that I've seen literally peel someone's skin off, is crying because I love him. I'm so stupid. I lean into his body to wipe those tears away, peppering his face with kisses. The fact that this little angel before me has clearly never been shown the love he deserves wrenches my heart nearly in half. He has been nothing but honest from the start. He isn't like any other man I've met.

"I knew it would be you," he said kissing me tenderly before he lays back bringing me with him. He covers us with the blankets still tousled from this morning. We lay like that in the silence as the sun rises. "I love you too, My Dove," he whispers into my hair, kissing my head as I fall asleep; finally feeling like the sprint has ended.

CHAPTER 16

I woke up in the middle of the day, our night. This schedule has my system incredibly messed up. I look up at Asmodeus who is already awake, sitting there watching me, probably the real cause of me waking up. Still groggy and not ready to talk I drape myself over his chest to trace the lines of his body.

"What is this?" I finally break the silence, running my fingers over the intricate swirls covering his bicep and up his collarbone earning a shiver from him.

"When Lui and I decided to go full renegade and rage against our system." He smirked down at me, waggling his eyebrows, clearly being goofy. "We wanted something to make us distinctive. There really are no tattooists outside of the singular shaman in this market, and he tattoos 'as the gods will it.' So we sat through the pieces and now we have something to always remember what we're fighting for."

"So, you knew each other before this?"

"Lui was my best friend from the time we were created."

I sit in silence for a minute, thoughts swirling. "What are you fighting for?" I tuck my hand under my chin looking up at him. He sighs.

"I'm the youngest of five," Asmodeus starts his story, "usually the gods will it so that those that wield water are born first, they're meant to be the leaders of their houses because they're usually the most dangerous. Somehow though our cycle started wrong, with earth, fire, light, air and then me. My family was concerned as the youngest I would have problems with my inheritance going to what they considered a weaker sibling. I never really wanted anything to do with them though, I grew up seeing how they treated humans as little more than the bottom dwellers. I saw the deals we were making with the humans in power to make sure it stayed that way and I refused to continue being complicit in it. Lui got into a scrape, and it wasn't even a thought, I went with him. I moved out to the woods skirting the bog lands, as far from my family as I can get without leaving the darkness completely." He finishes his story with a firm nod, so much clearly missing but just enough for me to understand why he is the way he is.

"Could you leave the darkness?" I wonder aloud processing this little snippet of family history.

"Hypothetically yes, but I can't see well. Humans think the light hurts us when really, we're just blind in it." His eyes crinkle as I giggle, I should have figured.

"Would you want to live in the light, Dove?" He looked worried, realizing for the first time I might not want to live at night.

"No, definitely not. I'd prefer to stay with my friends." I sigh content. Closing my eyes, I put my ear back to his chest, listening to his heartbeat as I go back to tracing his tattoo with my fingertips.

"There's really no one else you would care to see?" His voice is quiet below me, but he sounds sad.

"Again, definitely not. I have a great-aunt that I was living with in name only that was already knocking at deaths door and an elderly professor that gave me my dagger. Neither of them were very good to me and I doubt either of them are expecting to see my face again." I think of the few people in our town I would see daily but the only one I firmly remember is Kallum. I'll never forget his stupid face.

Noticing my shift Asmodeus looked down at me, gripping my chin in his too long fingers to make me look up at him. "Someone hurt you." He looked angry.

"A lot of things hurt me." I stayed in his hold looking into the constellations before me.

I told him about my earliest memories. My mother singing to me before she just wasn't there anymore. I tell him about hunting and running through the woods with my father. About him being taken when he opposed the prison wagons and The Summit, specifically. How he raged against the guards as they loaded him up into the wagon. He thrashed into the one holding him, breaking his nose. I couldn't do anything but hide in the trees and watch, following the prison wagon most of the way out of town before they pulled over. That same guard grabbed a rock from the road and bashed his head in, still shackled.

He holds me a little tighter and I take a second to breathe through the memory. I've never even told Libby that part of the story, always choosing to say I just never saw him again. I tell him about meeting Libby and how much her friendship changed my life. How her mother would always weave crystals in my hair when I could be convinced to come in 'just for a moment'. Libby continuing the tradition well after her death. Then I start to tell him about Kallum and the clouds in his eyes turned to hurricanes. I wasn't scared of Kallum, not at first; but my lack of fear didn't make my self-esteem immune to the beating it would take from him.

When his family migrated to the woods around our towns center, we were only six. They were one of the few surviving families after The Rift opened in their town. We would play in the woods together all the time and I started to form a crush on him I couldn't shake. We hit ten and everything changed. He was constantly making fun of my eyes and pulling on my braid, until he started shunning me completely.

There were only a few boys and girls in our towns school at the time it was established, and my body seemed to be the only one rounding out. My cleavage would never stay in the band meant for it and shirts never fit right. The older I got the more he started to talk to me again though, almost trying to form a friendship.

It all came to a head after we had turned 16. He had started being so kind, almost gallant, walking us to the edge of Edna's estate each day. It was like he was a completely different person, until he wasn't. He saw me in the woods one day when I was alone for once. He whistled, watching the swish of my hips as I walked to school. Late because Libby was sick, and I stayed in her yurt longer than I should have to make sure she was taken care of. He had to have stayed in the woods waiting for me, finally seeing his opportunity. I turned confused by the sound, especially upon seeing who it came from. I was only scared for that split-second, choosing to turn and walk faster.

He reached out, grabbing my ass before I whirled on him. I tried to strike him, but he caught my hand, bending my wrist back to bring me to my knees. My heart was pounding and everything was moving so fast I can barely remember how it happened, but in a blink he was on top of me. I just barely got a grasp on one of my father's throwing knives as he tried to rip my pants off me. In a panic I swiped the knife in front of me, marring the side of his face. I scrambled out from under his body, his blood dripping onto my shirt. Standing, panting, I whirled around, knife firmly in hand.

"If you ever touch me again that will be your throat," I seethed at him gesturing to his wound with the knife as he cursed, gripping his gushing face.

"If I realized it was an ogre I wouldn't have touched it in the first place," he spat at me, and it shouldn't have, but the disgust on his face did something to my heart. Made me realize just how far someone would go to get what they want. The nickname stuck, even though he was the monster roaming those woods.

"So, we kill him." Asmodeus' voice brings me back to reality.

"Excuse me?"

"So. We. Kill. Him." He repeated slowly like I was crazy for not understanding him.

"You'd do that for me? Take me back there and exact vengeance on my nemesis?" I waggle my eyebrows up at him, mimicking his earlier expression.

"I would raze your town to dust if it would make you happy," he murmured and suddenly I can only focus on his lips.

The idea of him killing for me shouldn't be a turn on, yet here I was slowly shifting my thighs to create a little bit of friction. The idea of him turning his feral rage on the people who hurt me giving me a sick sense of satisfaction. This avenging angel was all mine. I press a kiss to his collar bone glancing up at him through my lashes.

He was staring down at me hungrily; and just like that the conversation was over. We seem to be meeting on the same page frequently these days.

I slowly begin a trail of kisses down his muscular torso and pause chuckling to myself. His buckle and the button of his pants were still undone. Right as I went to remove the last barrier to what I've been fantasizing about for weeks my fingers won't move.

"Take your clothes off first." He demands, releasing my fingers. I want to huff at him in frustration but this time I won't leave room for his form of scolding; I'm going to do exactly what he asks. I'll just do what he asks on my own terms. I stand slowly peeling my pants off, allowing my shirt to billow around my hips blocking everything he was looking for. I kicked my pants to the side to look at the being before me, his eyes glued to the hem of my shirt, barely covering my mound. He's practically drooling.

Slowly, I start to lift the fabric. Inch by inch. I can feel his gaze burning a trail up my body as I finally pull it off to toss it next to my pants. I crawl back onto the bed, taking up my position kneeling beside his legs. I go right for his pants. I'm sick of waiting, and his procrastination is starting to get suspicious; his blood wielding so good I've never even gotten a glimpse of an outline. I get his pants shimmied down about an inch before I need to give him a look.

"Oh, did you want help princess?" He grins at me, before pushing his pants off and to the floor. He lays back and I choke, there's no way that is supposed to fit inside of me.

I know what I was planning but I'm going to have to make some adjustments. I kneel between his legs, my hair brushing his thighs. His cock is perfect, if such a thing could exist. I lean forward and run my tongue up the underside of his shaft, eliciting a groan that has my toes curling. I wrap one hand around his base and run the flat of my tongue over the liquid beading up at the tip, the taste of him nearly enough to finish me right there. This time I groan as I suck the tip of him into my mouth swirling my tongue, trying to lap up every ounce of him. I start to sink my mouth down when I feel him scooping my hair up, transferring it to one hand.

His grip is almost painful as I bob my head, seeing how far I can take him down my throat. Using his grip on my hair he roughly pushes me down and I eagerly open for him as he rips my head back; a trail of saliva still connecting my mouth to the head of his member.

"So beautiful." He nearly growls pulling me up his body gently by my hair, forcing me to straddle his hips, so he can kiss me. I'm so distracted by the feeling of his manhood brushing my clit as he kisses me aggressively that it takes my breath away when he corkscrews his arms around my waist, breaking the kiss to flip me over, my thighs resting on his shoulders. His hands move to firmly grip my hips, his elongated fingers nearly wrapping completely around my thighs. He runs his tongue all the way along my slit in one smooth languid movement and I turn my attention back to my treat.

He has his face absolutely buried in my pussy and his cock down my throat and nothing in this world felt so right. He's using his hold on my hips to adjust me as he likes but I refuse to get caught up in the sinful things his split tongue is doing to my clit, keeping my time. I utilize the distraction to relax my throat for the mild pummeling its getting as he drops me down onto him. His concentration starts to slip, and his head lolls back. I pick up the pace, smiling to myself. Thinking I've won, I hum along his shaft until he adds a finger to my channel, the unused muscles latching onto his finger changing my hum to a near scream.

There's no pain, just indescribable pleasure as he strokes my inner walls using the arm he moved to wind around my waist to help me keep my pace. We are in a frenzied race to see who will give up and become absorbed by their pleasure first, barreling for release together. The ropes of his cum coat my tongue, the taste of him sending me over the edge of my own climax. I swallow every drop greedily, wanting to burn the taste of him into my memory.

We sit there for a moment panting before Asmodeus flops back onto the bed, all the air whooshing from his lungs and within a minute he's peacefully snoring, face still inches from my exposed labia. I laugh to myself, crawling up next to my knight to fall asleep peacefully in his arms. This time not waking until after sunset to travel the market again in search of Libby.

CHAPTER 17

We start working through the stalls as soon as we wake, and Asmodeus resumes his vigor for shopping for our home. His fingers interwoven in mine, we meander the market. He stops to talk to a human from the looks of it, an old woman with a nearly bald head, the white strands left poking up at every angle. He points to an orb on the wall behind her, almost like a crystal ball and she nods before he steers me away.

"I think that will be something you will like." He grinned, but before I could give him a sarcastic response, I see a stall full to the brim of stones and crystals. My mouth dries out and my legs are moving before I can even register it.

"That's where she is," I whisper, walking toward the shop in the corner. When we reach the stall, I take in the tables full of gems and raw stones. There was no one there but the very essence of the little shop screamed Libby. The canvas walls had tapestries stitched to them at interesting angles making an abstract wallpaper. Asmodeus strode for the back like he knew exactly what he was looking for and I strolled through taking in her wares, stopping at the last table before the stall ended.

There was a sculpture made of raw crystals somehow twisted together to make an unmistakable circlet of daisies. My heart was in my throat, the stall even smelled like her now that I was further inside. The scent of roses and rain and fresh earth overriding the incense throughout the market. The smell of Libby.

A clatter has me turning my head and there she is, Asmodeus grinning so widely behind her I think his cheeks might split. I take in my friend for the first time in nearly a month now. Her tiny body looked much stronger, lined with dainty muscles. Her honey eyes had bled red, the eyes that had looked up at me a million times crimson now. She had the tiniest red horns barely poking through her curly hair, but I couldn't see anything else different about her. Not that I could really see anything as my eyes filled with tears. For the first time since we left for the woods I broke down and cried. My body is completely wracked by sobs, and I feel my tiny friend squish me by the midsection the way she always used to.

I laugh at the sensation I never thought I'd feel again. I squeeze her back, my arms wrapping around her head and neck to smother her in love; resting my face against the crown of her head, her horns poking into my collarbone. We held each other rocking viciously, and by the time we pulled back we were both laughing, the crystals still woven in her chest length curls clattering against my arms. Being so much closer I can see her tiny wings now, jutting out like a mangled butterfly and the longforked tail knocking stones off the tables behind her. I chuckle, it just seems so Libby. She sobered up as I studied her, backing away further into her shop.

"Liberty, where the hell do you think you're going?" I chase her retreat through the shop and upon realizing I'm following her, she stops. Looking up at me wide eyed.

"You're not mad?" she whispered. what? I'm not mad? She's not mad? I think we both interpreted what happened to get us here incorrectly.

"Libby. Why would I ever be mad at you? If anything, I thought you were mad at me." I laugh as she just stares at me.

"Why would I be mad at you?" She asks but she looks mad now, her face scrunching up like it always used to. "Should I be mad at you?" She glares up at me and I giggle.

"Okay, I think we've established that no one's angry, and I'm rather interested in hearing this story." Asmodeus chimes in behind my friend, eagerly glancing between the two of us.

"We're going to need some drinks for that," Libby stated, disappearing to the back without another word. Asmodeus came to wrap an arm around my waist snuggling me into him, leaving me standing there wondering what I could have possibly done to have gotten so lucky.

***

"Alright," Libby said, taking her place at the small table we were now crowded around. We were in a small back room, the canvas of the back wall splitting to reveal a small lounge area. She had three cups set out with two fingers of a liquid that matched her old eyes. She drank her glass in one large gulp, pouring another and drinking that too before she starts.

"When we were in the woods, I figured out pretty quickly that we weren't going to make it where we were supposed to. I figured maybe we would get lost and travel a few days before we found a nice spot to settle on our own. I was sitting by the fire, finishing the hankie I was working on for your birthday when this tiny green thing comes hauling ass out of the forest straight for me. It grabbed my hair and pulled me through the brush, getting us far from the trail. It's the craziest thing, even though it was half the size of me I couldn't break away. It eventually dropped its hold on my hair. I thought I had just gotten too heavy for it," she recounted, her eyes darkening.

"But it wasn't tired. It was scared of the massive demon waiting on the trail. The terror I felt in that moment was unlike anything I've ever experienced, and I went into a frenzy. The details are so murky, I don't really remember anything until I regained my sanity and suddenly, I had a tail and..." She drops her face into her hands, taking a second to collect herself. Looking back up at me she said, "I fought him. Lui, I mean. I managed to ram him into a tree so hard his horns got stuck, and he had to rip them out." I stared at her mouth nearly touching the floor and Asmodeus sips from his cup of whatever chuckling.

"All he said was, I like the cut uh yer gib, I think I'll be keepin you." She mimicked Lui's accent terribly. "I didn't stop fighting him the entire time he carried me here; it was so bad I had torn my skirt and lost everything I collected. By the time we hit the ground I had done a number to his face and chest with my headbutts, and scratches, and he looked at me like he found his god wandering the woods." She finished cheeks flushing at the memory. So, it was true.

"Anyway, he set me up with my little stand, and he's been with me ever since; helping me however I needed it, even when my power was more uncontrolled." She finishes, obviously leaving a whole lot out. Taking after her I take a gulp of the liquid in my cup sputtering and choking as it blazed its way down my esophagus. What is this? Asmodeus nearly jumped out of his skin at the sound and Libby laughed. I look at my friend, realizing so much more has changed than just her appearance.

"So, you just, turned into a demon?" I ask slowly, still recovering from the liquid trying to scorch me from the inside out. Asmodeus now far too entertained by my brush with death. I was just trying to understand what had happened beyond Asmodeus' guesses. Libby giggled.

"Yes, but the demon was already there, inside me. Demons were already here before the main rift opened; my father was one of the first to migrate through to start making a home for them. That's why my mother refused to talk about him. We know how scatterbrained I am, I think she was just worried the truth would slip out someday, and she didn't know how else to keep me safe..." She trailed off, probably thinking about the father she never got to know.

"And you have a power you said?" I try changing the subject, not wanting to see the sad look in my friends' eyes get any deeper.

"Yeah, earth." She says simply, shrugging her tiny shoulders.

Asmodeus chokes on his drink this time, staring wide-eyed at the tiny imp in front of us who can't seem to keep a straight face.

"And that's.... bad?" I ask, confused by Asmodeus' reaction.

"When Lui brought you here, he came and got me, hoping when the timing was right, I could open the door so you could escape. We figured out early on that my powers were stronger than usual and opening the pod doors was almost second nature to me. I didn't know it was you until I saw you tearing the room apart piece by piece. I wanted to run in and grab you but when you locked eyes with me and gave me the finger." She stopped clearly very shaken by the memory.

"I realized that I had essentially just left you and had become exactly what you had been trying to defend me against." I can't stop the insane giggle that leave my lips at her words.

"Libby, I didn't see you, I was staring at Asmodeus." Who I'm realizing knew her because she had also been outside my window. That was why he was so confused about my friend being a human, because she wasn't.

"The day Ass went in for you, I waited until the market quieted and opened your pod. Lui vouched for him enough that I knew he would keep you safe and watching him wait outside your window was starting to get a little pathetic. I stayed tucked in between the stalls until I saw him racing away with you over his shoulder. I watched until I knew you had made it safely out. If I had known, you have to know I would have gone with you. I thought you wouldn't want to be around me." She starts picking at the wood on the table, her eyebrows furrowed in memory.

"I understand. It worked out for the best though, you found Lui." I nudged her leg under the table with my foot.

"I did, I also have a shop I love and a cute little hut just outside the nearest town, but I don't plan to stay there if you all are leaving. I never want to be far from you again. Besides, we wouldn't want his highness over there losing his head." She gestured to Asmodeus. His already pale face turned stark white. Why did she say that? No.

"You're joking," I say, eyes darting between my friend and my knight. Not knight. Fucking prince.

"ooop," lippy said covering her mouth with both tiny hands but the grin under them is unmistakable. "Was she not supposed to know that little tidbit?" she waggled her eyebrows at Asmodeus who glared at her with hell-fire behind those black eyes. The look he was giving her would have had me worried, if Lui didn't pick that exact moment to walk into the space.

"I think all three of you have some serious explaining to do." I tried my best to look as angry as I felt but with the two people I love most in front of me at last, it's kind of hard. Not to mention how distracting the insane amount of information that was just casually thrown at me was.

"Okay, yes I'm a prince." He spits the word out like it offended him. "though I swear I said that word would only be uttered under penalty of death." He gave a very pointed glare at Libby who just rolled her eyes at him. Clearly used to his theatrics by now. "But in name only. I have no desire to run a continent of humans, demons and hybrids."

"I'm sorry humans and demons?" I can't keep up with this anymore.

They quickly give me a rundown, both Asmodeus and Lui are filling each other's gaps to paint a pretty daunting picture. Basically, when they came through The Rift their royalty made a deal with ours. Their houses would be bound together and in repayment for the power the demons gave them, the men were to act as figureheads using the humans as a way to keep bloodlines going. The Summit wasn't for humans. Libby and I would have been set to end up matched to demons anyway. They were using us to build their empire and hiding it behind the guise of a rebuilding the civilization we lost. They needed the men strong and the women docile to ensure their plan worked, and given the curriculum, work it did.

Lui was bred to be Asmodeus' bodyguard and As took too much of a liking to him, that's the real reason they ran. His love for his friend what started this. I am fuming as I sit in the silence once they finish speaking. They only give me a brief synopsis of their history, not being in a safe enough environment to really get into it still in the crowded demon market; I was already sick to my stomach, finally starting to understand the world around me.

"There has to be something we can do." I rage, standing from my chair, flipping it backwards.

"There actually may be something." Libby's cheeks lift in an evil grin that has me second guessing this idea.

CHAPTER 18

Libby walks us through her little plan, cleaning up her shop as the sun started rising. Lui chuckles beside her, watching her with blatant cute aggression as she walked us through what we're retrieving.

"Okay, so we know any extensive Intel would have to be on paper, obviously coded. If we can get the actual information, it shouldn't take long for Lui to translate it." She looked up at him lovingly as she moved through her shop, placing her wares in a massive burlap sack.

"I do have me a way wif words," he grumbles at her shrugging, causing all of us to chuckle.

"So, we're just looking for papers?" I ask confused.

"Yes, if we want to know how deep this goes. We only have theories, we need proof. Especially if you want any hope of stopping this," Libby said resolute, looking at Asmodeus. He takes over her thought.

"They'll have to travel through the market to get into the heart of the kingdom." I shake my head still completely baffled. "We need to be looking for someone that's a part of the imperial army."

As if the gods themselves had been listening, an orange demon wearing nothing but black walked by. The uniform exactly the same as the ones the humans outside our school wore. Asmodeus laughed, nudging me to point him out. I went to look over at Libby and realized she had already ducked through the fabric at the back of her stall.

"Sneaky nymph that un." Lui shook his head in appreciation as there was a great whooshing and the earth rumbled so hard the stones left went clattering off the tables, followed by complete silence. The men walked out before me, whooping in the direction of the guard that had vanished as they turned the corner. For the first time in quite a while I'm scared to see what awaits me.

I hesitantly walk around the corner of the tent and my mind immediately blanks. I couldn't understand the sight before me, my tiny best friend perched in an oak tree that hadn't been there minutes before. She was grinning madly down at us and then I saw it, a small hole in the trunk of the tree, the orange demon pacing inside of it furious. My jaw dropped to the ground as she jumps down to land butt first in Luis massive hands. It was like they had done this dance a million times before. He set her down gingerly, trailing her as she walked to the hole in the tree. It was a bit too high for her, she scrunched up her nose in frustration before a massive toadstool grew right under her feet, providing her a little landing to see into the tree.

The demon was trying to burn the tree from the inside out, but Lui was putting out the fires every time they would take hold. Fire went flying directly at her face and Libby actually giggled as it parted just short of her nose.

"Please, keep it up. Fire is foreplay for us." She winks at the orange demon, and he noticeably paled. What happened to her?

I watched Lui, Asmodeus and Libby stand at the tree from the safety of the stall. Turning into a demon and losing her frailty had turned my friend into a bad ass. I sat back reveling in their mayhem until they were finished, and the boys came waltzing back. Asmodeus playfully punched Lui as they walked and Lui gave him a shove in response that sent Asmodeus flying across the market. As stood up, black eyes darkening and ran for the demon headfirst. He barreled into his legs knocking them both over, taking the fight to the ground, nothing but a flurry of stark white and burgundy limbs.

"They'll probably be at that a while." Libby rolled her eyes, taking my hand to lead me back into her shop. I looked back at the tree over my shoulder to see that the hole had closed leaving the demon inside. My stomach bottomed out a little bit, I feel so out of my depth.

"If you're feeling bad for that one, don't. I saw what happened to the last girl he bought," Libby said, spitting into the dirt in the trees direction and pulled me into her stall. I instantly felt better knowing he wasn't just some random guy caught at the wrong time.

"So, you're branded." Libby gestures to my arm, the silence has never been so loud.

"Kind of, yes? We made an arrangement. He fulfilled his end of the bargain, but he hasn't asked me to do the same yet."

"You bargained with him for your essence? You didn't just fall head over heels for that narcissistic charm and want to be bonded to him forever?" She laughed to herself.

"Yeah, I told him he could have my soul if he helped me find you and- "

"Excuse me?" Libby said her lip wobbling, looking up at me like she could see into my mind. "You made a deal with the devil to find me and save me? Not even knowing if I was alive?" Her tears were falling.

"Of course." I stop to really look at my best friend as she is now, not as she was. "I love you Libby, I'll always come for you." And then were both crying. How fitting that our partners are outside beating each other to hell while we're inside holding each other through a torrent of tears.

"We can get you out of this, Bryn," Libby whispered, panicked once the worst of the tears had receded.

"What?" I laughed down at her sniffling.

"You made a stupid choice in a hopeless situation. You don't have to give it to him, we can figure out a way around it. I'll help you, if that's what you want." She was looking at me with so much conviction, I knew she would do whatever I asked her to do without a question.

"No, Libby. I want this." My laughter stopped with the heating of my face, and she just stared at me open-mouthed as my face deepened to the same color as Lui's skin.

"Told ya they're a match from the pit itself." Lui smirked at her, walking in fully bloodied and I panicked for a split-second before my prince followed in spotless, adjusting his shirt. He was smiling at me like I was the sun he revolved around. I ran over to plant a kiss firmly on his mouth, relieved he was unscathed. I turned just in time to see Libby lick a blood trail from Lui's face. She scrunches her freckled nose, dramatically gagging in distaste.

"That's not yours," she pouts from his arms almost completely smothered in his embrace. I whirl on As to check for wounds again thinking I missed something, when I remember his absolutely insane healing ability. He noticed my overreaction though and his smile some-how grew wider.

"Worried about me, Dove?" He boops my nose play-fully like he so often does and wraps his arm around me to pull me into his side.

Libby began speaking from Luis hands which have been settled into place at his chest to form a little elevated throne for her just below his face. She looked like a fallen fairy queen, with her tattered red wings that I've yet to see her use.

"So, we have gathered that the information about the human side of The Summit should be coming in via the main trails within the next few days."

"Why would they move information so publicly like that? Are they really that cocky?" The people in charge don't seem very smart but seeing that for once I'm the fragile one and don't really know anything about their kind, I have no problem leaving the main planning up to them.

"Who would ever dare oppose father?" Asmodeus' feral grin reflected in his eyes, and I remembered exactly why I fell in love with him. "It does seem a little strange though. Father got this far because of his caution. Only making dramatic moves once all the pieces were in place. Either this is worse than we thought, or something has happened." I shift further into his hold as he finishes.

They go on discussing where the group transporting the information should be by now. The Summit only would have officially ended about three weeks ago, and given the time to accumulate the numbers on the humans and where they ended up shipped off to, they should only be a day or two from the main gates. We quickly got to work packing the rest of Libby's wares into the large sack, big enough for Lui to carry slung over his shoulder for her. The second we had her stall squared away, we set out on the road trying to intercept whatever information we could get.

Safely out of sight of the gates, Libby trailed off into the bog where she set all the treasures from her shop on the ground before binding them in a ball of vines and moss and letting the ground absorb it.

"I'll be back for you." Libby kissed the air toward the disappeared vine ball and skips back to us. Asmodeus has scooped me up into his strong arms and I rest my head on his shoulder, the same way I had before everything came together. Libby glared at Asmodeus like she would snuff out his very existence herself if he so much as breathed on me wrong, before she scampered over to Lui who had lowered a hand for her to kneel on, boosting her up to sit on his shoulder through the worst of the bog.

CHAPTER 19

W e walked through the boggy woodlands in relative silence; listening for the imperial demons we were meant to be looking for. I would be lying if I said I wasn't being lulled into a sleep with each step Asmodeus took, Libby didn't seem to be faring much better. She was still perched on Luis shoulder with one tiny arm slung up to wrap around one of his horns in an effort to stay steady as she dozed against the side of his face, her small torso fitting perfectly against his massive cheek. The size difference between them was downright comical but the obvious love they had for each other had my heart skipping beats for her.

His big golden orbs kept ticking over toward her to check on her position and make sure she wasn't slipping. He looked like he was about to adjust her when her little red rimmed eyes shot open, grinning at Lui. He visibly jumped at the sudden change, and we all chuckled a bit as he cleared his throat and removed her from his shoulder, setting her on the ground gently.

"I may or may not have been setting little tripwires as far as I can on the trail ahead of us every so often, and one may or may not have just been tripped." She grinned savagely. Truly incredible.

"Okay so what's the plan this time?" I ask not wanting to sit out. Asmodeus gives me a worried look and Libby's smile falters a little.

"I don't want you to get hurt Bryn, our bodies are built different," Libby said gently. I knew that, I knew that a scratch to them was death to me, but I don't want to just spend the rest of eternity as the damsel in distress.

"When we make our exchange, you'll be a little sturdier and then you can come on all the dangerous missions," Asmodeus said almost reading my mind. He chuckled as he crooned the last part of his sentence pinching both my cheeks in his hand, screwing my lips up before he quickly sobered up. "I can't lose you." He let go of my cheeks to cup the side of my face and for a second, I let him; fully prepared to sit this one out until an idea hit me like lightning. I straighten looking at my best friend.

"Libby, it took you a moment to grow that tree out of nowhere. How long will it take you to entangle a group of people?" From the look on her face, longer than she would have without someone attacking.

"Asmodeus, they know who you are, and they very well probably would know Lui. There's no way you're intercepting them on this trail without an immediate fight and possibly losing information." Asmodeus is looking at me like he did the day I tried to talk to him sealed in that stone, in absolute wonder. "I want to help," I say firmly with a resolute nod at all of them.

"Okay then." Libby eyes As wearily before looking into my eyes. "Lead on."

***

It didn't take long for us to get into our positions. I was standing smack dab in the middle of the trail with a fire roaring at my feet, Libby and As tucked away among the foliage, Lui airborne to make sure there aren't any surprises as we deal with the demons coming our way. We had it on pretty good authority, thanks to Libby's insane earth abilities, that there were four of them. I sit myself down, trying to make myself small. The four demons finally came up on the trail ahead of me. Their movement slowed seeing my fire but not stopping as they realized it was just me sitting there.

"What've we got ere?" A massive green demon, like the last one I killed, spoke first. I try my best to stop my eye from twitching in anger and shrink back to make myself smaller, earning a chuckle from the entire gang. They move closer, right into the area I'm sitting where the trails bottleneck ends causing it to fan out slightly. I can't stop my lips from ticking up as they get closer and I start to feel Asmodeus power trickle into me through the brand. The adrenaline coursing through me honing my focus.

They didn't even get close enough to touch me. Once I could firmly feel all four bodies around me, I put everything into stopping them in their tracks. Libby and As far enough out to avoid me accidentally grabbing them too. They wouldn't have had to worry though because holding the four that I'm holding completely still is taking absolutely all of my effort. The ground rumbles as roots from the surrounding trees launch themselves from the ground to wrap around two of the demons' legs, pulling them down into the dirt.

I focus my energy on the two still standing in front of me frozen, eyes widened in terror at the human before them. Completely at my mercy. This was too easy. I can't stop the giddy laugh that falls from my lips as Libby's tree roots take firm hold of the two left in front of me. She made quick work of burying all four of them in the dirt. Asmodeus exits the foliage once they're all firmly entombed up to their chests, arms trapped to their sides, swaddled in individual balls of roots.

"Hello boys," he drawls, slowly taking his power back through the brand. Lui lands in the opening of the path beside As and the ground shudders with the impact. All four of them, although no longer under thrall, are completely frozen, wide-eyed.

Libby grabs my arm to pull me away, but my feet stay firmly rooted as I watch my prince take the knife that he keeps in his boot to the face of the demon in the ground furthest to the right. Watching him work, my core heats in a way that it really shouldn't. His surety of himself and delicate precision with the blade is enchanting. I sit there chewing on my lip barely even realizing Libby was yanking my arm trying to pull me back into the woods. Libby pulls harder finally speaking.

"Bryn, I don't want you to see this, please." I look back at her desperate face as she pulls me toward where the woods are almost too dense to walk. "I want to show you something!" Her face lights up with an idea and I finally move, following her through the wood, but not before taking one last glance back to the god of wrath bound to me.

CHAPTER 20

Libby led me tripping through the dense foliage until all we could hear was a cacophony of bugs. Only stopping when my feet started slowly sinking into the ground. She flitted effortlessly over the mud with her little wings, and I watched her in awe as she built me a little landing to stand on out of vines, weaving them together beneath me.

"Watch," she said, face scrunching up in excitement.

There was a slight rumbling and ten stalks shot up toward the sky, coming up almost to my nose. Each giant tulip like bulb a different mixture of colors. The one closest to me bloomed open, the variegated purples and greens stealing my breath. Where the Pistil of the flower should be there was a small crystal nestled into it. It looked like the flower had grown the little gem. Libby squealed in delight as they opened one by one, every color imaginable and collected the corresponding crystals. She finally landed in front of me on the vine landing she had fashioned and held the crystals up to me.

"Do you want some?" She shook her hand, waggling her eyebrows as the stones clattered. I picked an onyx with rainbows that shoot from it when it hits the light, just like Asmodeus eyes.

"You've got it bad," she says, clicking her tongue as she deposits the rest of the stones into the pocket of the flowing sage skirt she wore. She had embroidered tiny little flowers along the hem, fixing the hole in her pocket from her fight with Lui with brightly colored thread; the rainbow catching my eyes.

I realized I haven't spoken since our plan worked, my mind just a constant whirl of new information.

"This is so cool, Libby. How are you able to do so much in such little time? This seems like magic." I smile down at the little rock in my hand, absolutely amazed.

"I don't really know, once the demon genes in me awoke I just kind of handled it." She shrugged. "These flowers were one of the first things I learned how to summon to me."

"Did you know that this was a possibility?" The idea that she kept this from me making my heart squeeze.

"I did. My mother never told me much about my father, but Lui thinks he was one of the main generals and I would have inherited my power from him when he passed. When she died, she told me about the warnings he gave her and the protection he gave us until they were found out. None of our stories seem to get much of a happy ending." Her voice matched the feelings swirling in my gut, the fact that she kept this from me put a hole through my chest.

"Are you okay?" Libby peered up at me, looking into my mind in the way she's always been able to.

"There's just a lot to adjust to. I came into this completely blind, and you knew and didn't tell me. You didn't trust me." My voice breaks on the last bit and her eyes have widened, already brimming with tears.

"Bryn, I'm so sorry. I never meant for any of this to happen. I promise I didn't know more than the absolute basics, and only information about my father specifically. It wasn't because I didn't trust you, I was ashamed. My people took everything from yours. Look at the mess were in." she gestures around her. "None of this would have happened if it weren't for the king and the men like my father." I wrap my arms around her as her tears finally spill over. It feels like we've lived lifetimes together. Pulling away, I look into her mostly red eyes.

"You get a pass on this one, but if you ever keep anything from me again, I'll lose it." I glare down at her as she nods viciously, drying up her tears.

"Never. No more secrets," she swears. We fall back into silence, and she grows more of those little flowers. Her flowy long-sleeved shirt slipping back just enough to reveal her brand.

"YOU SAID NO MORE SECRETS!" I grabbed her arm, pushing her sleeve back to take in the intricate mark. She just laughed.

"Okay, well I thought that would be assumed." I laugh with her, this time helping her collect the crystals from my little vine platform.

"I thought the brands were just a human-demon thing." My laughter stops, genuinely curious.

"No, in your case it is, because you're working on a deal. In our culture though it's just a much more intense marriage. A direct line to one another, two souls never to be apart again. It's a way to ensure forever, and in cases like ours adjusting things slightly so everything works as it should." She giggles to herself and given their size difference it's easy to guess exactly what she needed adjusted. We sat in silence, my face burning.

"I know you wanted to stay with him," Libby uttered nearly under her breath once the blood in my face had settled back down. "Listen Bryn, you're going to see a lot of things living in this world." She gestures to the bog around her. "I've rarely been able to help you, just let me protect you from the things that I can protect you from, please?" she was trying to preserve the innocence I still had. I realized that beyond Asmodeus charging from the market with me over his shoulder, she doesn't know anything that's happened.

"I've changed a lot too, Libby." I tell her about everything that happened on my end from her disappearance and once I reach the end, she's just staring at me.

"But you're human." she said as I finish telling her about the rogue demons on the road.

"Yeah, well when has that ever stopped me?" I grin down at her, and she gives me one of those evil little smiles I'm still getting used to. It hasn't been that long and yet everything has changed. We both stop smiling as we stare at each other realizing the person in front of us is vastly different from the person we lost that day in the woods.

"I'm still your best friend." Libby said almost reading my thoughts.

"Forever." I confirm grabbing her arm to loop it through mine as we start walking back toward the boys.

By the time I broke the tree line, the four demons were completely buried in the dirt, courtesy of Libby who flitted a bit ahead determined to not let me see the worst of it. I roll my eyes but can't help the warmth that floods my chest at her protectiveness. Lui was strapping the massive satchel the green demon had been transporting to himself as I came upon the clearing. Asmodeus' face lit up as he saw me walking back toward him. He grabs my face in both hands and kisses my lips firmly before pulling back to stare into my eyes.

"You are absolutely incredible." He kisses me again to punctuate it. Everything had gone smoothly, and Asmodeus had a backpack for each of us to add to our gear. I shoved my much smaller pack into the backpack I was given full of bound books. Libby slung her backpack on one of Lui's horns and perched herself back on his shoulder as we start walking again with our stolen information. Finders' keepers after all.

***

Asmodeus' home is quite a trek from the market, very near our old town. We walk all together trying to get back as quickly as possible. The forest isn't safe to pull any of our newly acquired goods out, and we're on borrowed time until they realize the Intel they're waiting for isn't coming. We're guessing we only have about three or four days before we have someone on our tail, and given my princes current renegade status they're going to come right for him.

The anxiety leaves a pit in my stomach, settling on the awareness that I can't do anything to protect him or Libby or even Lui, who I've grown shockingly fond of. Watching him dote on my best friend like she's the only thing on this planet helps, I'm sure. She stays almost exclusively on his shoulder wanting to be near him constantly. It was like they had this unspoken deep pull to each other, like neither was truly happy unless they were with the other.

I glance over at Asmodeus walking next to me. We haven't been alone since the hut a few days ago now and the walk has been busy enough to limit our time together to his brief stint carrying me. All our interactions recently have had to be so rushed and I find myself looking forward to getting to his home so the feeling of his arms around me wouldn't be a memory. I'm so lost in my thoughts, I startle when Libby finally speaks.

"So, what are you guys planning to do when we get back?" she breaks the silence with a devilish grin, and I flush nearly purple at the implication in her tone. She starts cackling, doubling over, nearly falling off Lui's shoulder. He grabs her and sets her on the ground.

"We both know you can't ride en talk little nymph." She laughed like this was a regular occurrence and matched her tinier strides to my own, keeping pace with me. She looped her arm through mine and Asmodeus looked over almost jealous of Libby's hold on my arm; like he was angry that she was touching me, and he wasn't. I glow under the attention and my friend tries again to start a conversation.

"Lui has been working on a little cabin not far from Asmodeus'. We're planning to move in there and finish it together now that he has the bones done. We'll never be more than a thirty-minute walk from each other." She smiled up at me, her face radiating genuine joy. I grinned down at her and glanced over at Asmodeus, who was smiling at me so tenderly my heart nearly leapt from my chest.

"Maybe we can even eventually 'acquire' some horses to make the trips faster." I smile down at her and her returning grin was just like being back in our old town, making mischief in the few ways we could. Now obviously on a much grander scale.

"Not that you aren't welcome, but I doubt you'll want to be anywhere near our home for quite some time," Asmodeus finally chimes in. The grin and wink he gives me making me choke, causing Libby to break into another fit of laughter.

"Maybe I do like this one," she laughed, and we kept walking. My heart singing between my favorite people.

CHAPTER 21

We traveled for another two days, stopping to laugh around the fire together; enjoying being in each other's company, knowing once we get back and decode the texts everything will likely change. It's amazing what feeling like you're on borrowed time will do for you. I've spent every second enraptured by my friends, choosing to live every second in my bubble of happiness until there's no other choice.

It seems like time is flying so fast it's giving me whiplash, but I suppose that's to be expected when everything you've ever known has been a lie. We reach Libby and Lui's home; a cute cottage built to Luis size needs. Libby hadn't seen the progress yet either and squealed in delight as the porch came into view, decorated in all the same herbs as her mother's yurt. He had assembled the outside of the building with stonework, creating a beautiful storybook pattern. It looked like a fairy tale.

"I got work to do still, don't get too excited," he grumbled at Libby as she ran up onto the porch, opening the door double her size without even touching it. The thick single slab of wood had been carved in the same pattern as the swirls along Luis horns.

Once we got inside it was bare, the vaulted roof making the small building feel much more open. There were the bones of three rooms, only one having its walls all the way up, and a large open space that will one day be a kitchen and living area, but it's very much unfinished still. A massive hearth was halfway mudded in the sitting room, clearly his main priority as a fire wielder. The floors were dusty, and his tools lay discarded around the space, as if Lui thought he would have much more time before bringing her here.

Libby was rocketing through the house, her skirt snapping behind her as she flitted from space to space talking about all the things they were going to do to make it their home, and my heart melted a little bit at my friends unbridled joy. Lui had also softened, her excitement easing the worry he had obviously been accumulating the closer we got. Grabbing a broom set in the corner I started sweeping, working through their kitchen. Everyone fanned out, picking a small thing to work on to clear the space enough for Lui to spread everything out while he works.

With four sets of hands, it wasn't long before the cottage was clean, the hearth was done, and we were dropping all the bags containing the stolen information in a pile in the empty great space for Lui to start reading through. I fished my pack out of the backpack I had been carrying, the much lighter bag a welcome relief. Libby, finally content with her space, came to stand in front of me.

"If you guys leave soon you can still make it to his house before dark." Her eyes glinted with mischief, we clearly weren't the only ones itching for some time alone. I grin down at her as she startles, remembering something.

"I never got to give you your birthday gift!" She said, running to the back room. I shook my head after her, the small unfinished handkerchief still tucked into my pack. She returned with a small bundle, pulling it from behind her back. She must have fished it out of Lui's bag once he had finally unclasped it. I unwound the fabric wrapping her gift and my eyes immediately started to well.

It was the small crystal sculpture of the circlet of daisies from her stall in the market, but she had taken some silver and replicated Asmodeus horns gracefully curling out of it. A piece of them both. I hugged her tightly, so grateful I get to call her my family and that we've found each other again. I just got my best friend back and yet here we are saying goodbye just over a week later. With a final parting squeeze, I turn back to Asmodeus who is trying very hard not to look impatient watching our exchange as he waits at the door.

"You better take care of her, Ass." She called out from behind me as I walked for him, scowling at him playfully.

"Until I am dust," he replied to her, holding out a hand to lead us home.

# CHAPTER 22

Just as Libby had said, it only took about thirty minutes of solid walking to reach Asmodeus' cabin. He had built it out of long logs painted black, sealing the wood against the elements. Brightly colored wildflowers contrasted the dark walls, wrapping the sides of the cabin in raised flower beds. The cheery yellows, pinks and oranges looking almost otherworldly against the dark background. The porch even had a small black swing hanging from the rafters to sit outside on and enjoy the woods around us.

"I had that installed for you," he said, noticing my attention catch on it and my heart fluttered.

He really thought of everything when we were in the market. The small handmade pillows sitting in the corners the same red as the tips of my hair. We walked into his home and my mouth fell open. The large sitting room was taken over by a giant fireplace, clearly designed by Lui. The stonework around the hearth a masterpiece itself. Two plush forest green velvet chairs flanked each side, making a perfect little reading nook in the main living space. A massive black fur rug took up almost the entire floor, it looked so soft I was scared to walk on it. The walls on the inside were the natural wood and it felt so cozy I wanted to curl up and take a nap right there.

He steers me through the log cabin gingerly. Pointing out a small kitchen just past the living area, fully stocked up and ready, the chairs and table like the one in my pod I had used as target practice. Looking over at the wicked amusement on his face I realize that was intentional. Hooks hanging from the rafters held pots and pans of varying sizes overhead, greenery looped along the ceiling, dangling down among the metal.

"Lui used to stay a lot, and he hated those." He gestured to the hanging cookware with a laugh. I couldn't stop my giggle at the mental image of Lui smacking into one face first. There was more than enough of everything we could need to stay here for a few months if we so desired. He leads me farther back to the only two rooms, which take up the entire back half of the space; like all he cared about was a decent sized bedroom. The small bathing room across from the main bedroom was just big enough for the huge bronze claw foot tub taking up the entire center.

"I wanted you to be able to enjoy it here." He seemed so insecure about me peeking through his space, as if wondering if it was good enough for me. Like he was worried this would be what breaks the deal.

"It's amazing As, thank you." I kiss him on the cheek lightly and this time he lets himself flush, finally feeling safe within the four walls of his home.

"That's not even the best part." He grins at me, before covering my eyes with his hands to show me the final area of our home. The bedroom was the biggest room in the cabin and managed to perfectly fit the gargantuan custom bed he had made for us. A black billowing canopy hung overhead, matching the furs on the over-sized mattress. There is another door in the corner which I can assume is a closet, and two small black tables on each side of the bed; the crystal ball he bought taking up much of the space on one. He had thought through everything, down to all the little things that would make my life here a functional and happy one. I can't stop my tears of unfiltered joy at having made it this far. I was looking at the posters of the bed he had made, the wood covered in the same swirling pattern as his horns, crying like an idiot, while this man stared on confused at my constant insane reactions to the situations I seemed to be finding myself in regularly. He wiped the tears from under my eyes and held my face in both of his hands to force me to look at him.

"You don't have to hold up your end, Bryn. I'll let it go," he murmured as the tears kept falling. "I just want you to be happy, even if that happiness is without me." His eyes were so sad looking down on me. He's misinterpreted my crying, thinking the tears were sad ones. I stared giggling and the sadness turned to the blank stare he so often gives when he gets too vulnerable or confused, trying to shut down the emotions he can't control.

"You upheld your part of the deal, I'll uphold mine." I stare into his black eyes looking for any sign of emotion and even though I'm talking about the deal, that's not what's keeping me here.

"Helping you find your travel companion was the decent thing to do. Seeing you find her was enough payment. I will never again see such joy." He ran his thumb over my cheekbones trying to memorize the feel of it. I don't like this one bit.

"And here I thought you weren't decent." I try to joke, but the look he gives me has a pit forming in my stomach. Why does this always seem to happen? I keep getting stuck in these situations I fear may make or break things with absolutely no idea what to say. I just look at him, mouth open trying to find the words to speak. Trying to figure out how to tell him I want to be with him more than I want the oxygen in my lungs.

"You don't need to explain Bryn." He lowered his hands and I wanted to throw up. The loss of his warmth like a part of me was taken. "I wouldn't want to be shackled to me; I can't do this to you," he said, so pained my heart splintered. He goes to move out of the bedroom, and I quickly grab his hand, pulling his arm to me.

"Why would you ever say that?" I'm mad, now that he's broken my panic spiral. How dare this sweet creature talk about himself like he's anything but a commodity. His brows furrowed at my scowl at him.

"I don't like when my friends talk badly about themselves." I scowl at him. "You had this entire place put together in a matter of what? Days? So, I would also feel at home here. You have done nothing but show me kindness and love and respect from the moment we met. You've proven time and time again that you would do anything to protect me including leave yourself vulnerable, so I could not be for once. That's decent Asmodeus. I'm so sick of people around me making decisions on the things that I want and the things that I can handle without ever taking a moment to consult me." I finish so frustrated I'm nearly yelling.

"So then, what do you want, Dove?" I can't see anything but the sparkle of hope in his eyes.

"You, idiot." I do yell then, as I grab that man firmly by both horns and kiss him with a desperation I didn't even know was there.

My face is wet. Am I crying? I pull back to look at my sweet prince, trying so hard to get the tears falling from his eyes under control. I can see them welling and then shrinking just to well up again. I put my hands on his face, my turn to wipe his tears.

"I want to be with you, for as long as we have, however that looks for us. If you don't want my soul that's a different story, but I still want to give it to you. Deal or no deal," I whisper at the end, the possibility of him not wanting me anymore finally hitting me.

"If we go through with this a lot of things will change-" He starts trying to explain but I cut him off.

"It doesn't matter. I'm sure." His smile is breathtaking, consuming me before his lips can, pushing me down onto the bed. He kisses my jaw lightly, before running the tip of his tongue down the length of my throat. I shiver in anticipation, but he pulls back to really look at me.

"I'm going to try to make this as painless as possible, I just need you not to fight me." He's staring into my soul with that gaze, like he's looking directly at his prize. "I need you to tell me you're one hundred percent sure. There's only so far into this were getting before you won't be able to back out anymore. "He looks so worried.

"Yes, I'm completely sure." I roll my eyes at him but make sure to hold his gaze as I say, "I'm not going to change my mind, Asmodeus. I've known for a while." I smile up at him still hovering over me on the bed. He smiles again but pulls away to crawl up the bed. He waves a hand over the crystal ball, and we're inside of a galaxy. The darkened room becoming a swirling cosmos around the bed.

I could count the constellations. I was completely breathless, just lying on the bed staring up at the twinkling stars before me in awe. He laid down next to me, also watching the stars. His bare arm brushing mine, he had taken his shirt off. I look over at his profile. The stars providing more than enough light to see every aspect of him clearly now. My eyes run down the rippling muscles of his abdomen, stopping on the bulge starting to tent the front of his pants. I bite my lip staring at him.

"I knew you would like it," he says, smiling to himself.

"Yeah, It's an incredible view." I keep my eyes firmly planted on him. As if sensing my stare, he looked over to make eye contact with me. Realizing what I was saying, his mouth opened with a small pop. I grin and move to straddle his waist. Staring down at his perfect face. All mine. I lean forward to lock our lips. No more procrastinating, I've never been surer about anything in my life.

The stars are shifting above me, and Asmodeus is shifting below me as I kiss him, grinding my hips against his. I sit up just long enough for him to pull my shirt off. He rips the band holding my breasts in two and my breath catches in my throat as he rolls us over to hover over me again. I'm still not used to being the weakest in a room and the way he touches me like I could break makes me want to smack him. I want him to hold me, to take advantage of just how much stronger he is, but he doesn't. He gently and tenderly kisses his way down my body to remove my pants, standing to survey is work.

"Incredible," he murmurs, peeling his own off; his cock springing past his belt line as his pants slide off his hips. My mouth waters, remembering the taste of him.

He strokes himself, standing over me, finally back in his home in the middle of the woods. All alone. He grabs my leg pulling me to the edge of the bed, spreading me before him. He slowly runs a single finger along my entrance.

"So wet, already?" He licks my honey from his finger, and I groan tracking every millimeter of his tongue. These games he plays will be the death of me.

I reach down to grip his length, running his head through my folds enjoying the friction. His eyes are so black they're sucking in the stars around them. He grabs my hand, holding firmly.

"I won't take your will this time but if you keep that up, I won't be gentle." He looked down at me, animalistic desire barely concealed as I moved him again, shifting to position him at my entrance.

"Good," I whisper, but the sound is cut off as he buries himself into me to the hilt. My muscles desperately loosen and contract trying to adjust to the sheer size of him. I see stars, joining the ones already floating in front of my face. He was completely still, staring down at where we were joined together with those black pits. He brings his hips back until all that's left is the tip of him inside of me and roughly buries himself again causing me to cry out. It hurts but the pain is so good, I never want it to stop. He pulls all the way out, checking me worriedly.

"Are you okay?" He's panting, trying to calm himself down and I'm pissed. I sit up and give his arm a good tug, toppling him over onto the bed.

He let me move him, probably thinking that was my way of asking him to stop. Instead of snuggling into him though, I perched myself back in his lap. Taking him entirely in one smooth stroke as I drop down onto him. Registering what was actually happening, Asmodeus' black eyes shoot open, his fingers gripping my hips hard enough to bruise and I love every second of it. I slowly start shifting my hips, enjoying the fullness and the friction. He seems to be straining to even breathe as I adjust, having him entirely at my whim.

Feeling a little less overstretched I lift myself all the way up before plopping down to bury him in me again, warmth shoots through me, and he groans; the sounds the closest I've ever heard him to being unrestrained, which is exactly what I want. I pick up my movement, earning sounds from him that have me barreling to my own release. I ride him through the stars until I'm tumbling through my own pleasure, trying to catch my breath. Asmodeus doesn't give me the chance, flipping us over, still connected.

"I like when you use me." He nips at my neck, hard enough to mark me and I shiver. "It's my turn now, Dove." All I can do is grab his back and one of his horns as he pounds into me, scooting us across the massive mattress until my head is hanging over the other edge. He wraps his fingers around my throat as he holds his pace, the lack of oxygen and the orgasm sitting right there have my head spinning when my entire body is on fire. Not in a cute way either, my nerve endings were being singed. The flames licking over every part of my body, dousing me in acid. I go to scream but the pain dies down almost immediately leaving a slight burn that's only enhancing the pleasure he's still ringing from my body.

"Such a good girl, taking it so well," he croons down at me, running the tip of his tongue down the length of my neck. That does it and I'm hurling over the edge of another orgasm. That sudden excruciating pain already completely forgotten, lost in Asmodeus. He's still going, milking out the last orgasm as long as he can. My body definitely still burns but the ache is fading with every second. He grins down at me.

"You're going to give me one more." He nips at my ear, and I don't even have the strength to lift my head up from the side of the bed. He scoots us down a bit, so I can rest my head comfortably and sits back on his heels.

Everything is so sensitive, every nerve ending heightened almost unbearably but as he starts moving again, I find myself bucking against him, doing exactly what he told me to. He grabs my hand, placing it on my clit, encouraging me to stroke myself as he watches from above. It almost looked like his eyes rolled all the way back for a moment, upon taking in the sight.

There's nothing but the stars and our breathing as we race the rest of the way to our climax. I go over the edge first, this time with a scream that nearly wrecks my vocal cords, as he pulls out. He gives his cock two more good pumps before his seed covers my torso, painting me in a masterpiece.

He simply falls to the side, burying his face in the furs on the bed. Both of us just lying in the absolute silence, trying to catch our breath. I'm lying there with my eyes closed, still covered in his cum when he chuckles next to me. I peek over at him, the room so bright I close my eyes again immediately. Day must have broken. I merely murmur in his direction, eyes still closed. His weight left the bed and when it returns two minutes later it is to wipe me up with a warm washcloth. So considerate. I try again to open my eyes, this time letting them adjust a bit to find Asmodeus grinning down at me. Standing at the edge of the bed, cloth still in hand.

"Immortality suits you well, Dove."

"Excuse me?" I said abruptly sitting up.

"You gave me the essence of your humanity; we're bound together forever. You agreed to this?" He questions, and his face starts to solidify. He's panicking, honestly rightfully so.

"No, no I know." I start trying to calm him when it hits me. "Wait. You said things will change…. Did you mean…. Me? I would change?" Libby had said the same, but I assumed that would have been because of his size.

His face is a complete mask as he says, "there's a mirror in the bathroom. I'm so sorry." He drops the cloth, burying himself in the blankets on the bed until he's completely shrouded. What a weirdo.

I am worried though as I cross the hall, I should have asked more questions, he tried to explain, and I wouldn't let him. I take a deep breath entering the bathroom, it'll be okay I tell myself, how bad could it actually be. I look in the mirror to a face that's recognizable but also not at all and have to hold back a yelp at the shock.

The burn wasn't like the initial brand, it had changed my entire body, I had become one of them.

CHAPTER 23

I could only stare at the creature in the mirror before me, open-mouthed, mimicking my every movement. Holy shit. This is a lot. This is so much. My once blue eyes were now the same black as Asmodeus', which explains the change in brightness. The small brown spot had leached blue, leaving a lake in the two black pits that were now my eyes. I glance up to see the slightly smaller silver ram like horns jutting from just under my hairline. My skin color paled to rival Asmodeus', nearly shimmering in the light of the bathroom. The only sound I'm capable of making, a confused whimper. This misunderstanding is entirely my fault and poor As is in a heap because of it.

I take a deep breath. This is okay. We can work with this right? I quickly spin. No wings and no tail. I let out a sigh of relief. I've apparently just become fully compatible with As. I still felt the same inside. I had probably been standing here looking in the mirror for an hour, adjusting to the changes. I expected to be a lot more freaked out than I was. After the initial shock, I've simply been just trying to learn this new version of me. I can keep up with him now, and he won't have to worry about me dying every two seconds. The bruises I'm sure his grip would have left already healed. This is a good thing, if I want to stay with him anyway and I absolutely do.

I run my fingers through my hair bumping my brand-new horns which sends a zing down to my toes. I look back toward As apologetically realizing how uncomfortable me grabbing his had to have been. I walk back into our bedroom, and he's still just a lump under the blankets. Completely unmoving. I can't blame him. With my track record if I was in his position I would have spontaneously combusted. He thinks this is his fault. I slowly lift the blankets, and he blinks an eye open at me, peering out from his little nest.

"It's safe to come out." I grin down at him, and he looks thoroughly confused. That seems to be how things go for us. He removed his still naked torso from the blankets and being able to totally see him even in the dark has my thoughts scattering.

"I like your blanket nest." I chuckle at him, trying to distract myself from how much I want to eat him alive.

"You're okay?" He's eyeing me like I'm going to have a breakdown. I've never been normal in these situations though, why would I rage at the fact that I finally stand a chance at holding my own in an unfair system.

"Yes, Ass. I'm fine." I shake my head at him, laughing, and he just stares at me in wonder.

"You truly are incredible, Bryn." He grabs my face studying me. Taking in the few changes just like I did. "Slightly insane, but incredible nonetheless."

I study him right back, taking him in with new eyes. I notice the brand on his arm matching my own, a direct line to each other, never to be apart again, just like Libby said. We sat there in silence until he reached up, stroking the length of one of my swirling new horns, causing my eyes to nearly cross at the sensation.

"I like these. Evens the playing field a little bit." He does it again and I smack his hand, the impact moving him for once. He shook his hand out squaring his jaw with a feral smile. "Oh, we're going to have fun, Little Dove."

I hurt him. Unintentionally at that. Yes. We indeed were going to have fun, I thought to myself as I launched into his relaxed form; unguarded now that his anxiety has calmed, tackling him to the mattress with a slew of kisses.

He laughed attempting to knock me off, but I held him down. I was strong for a human, I doubted this would be that different and I seemed to be right. His laughter stopped, and he looked at me angrily, thoroughly stuck under me.

"I thought we were having fun, Prince." I look down at him, grinning from my perch on his chest. His arms securely under my legs.

He tried one more time to shake my hold before stilling, taking in my body sitting on his chest like my own personal throne. I wasn't anticipating him leaning forward to dart his tongue into my folds, causing me to jerk just enough that he was able to flip me. Back to the mattress, face still between my legs Asmodeus grinned up at me.

"Oh, we are." He purred licking slowly along my seam. "Don't you think, Dove?" He nips my thigh and I jump incapable of responding. "I thought so." He ate me within an inch of my orgasm and as he pulled away, I nearly screamed in frustration. Stopping just short of where I needed him to be. He stands fisting himself.

"Let's see if this pretty cunt can't take more of a beating now." He said sliding into me, my eyes rolling back into my head. I thought he was lost before but that was his gentle. Now that he's not as worried about breaking me he is truly unhinged. Pounding into me mercilessly. My gasps, turn to moans, turn to pleas when I start to smell smoke.

"Shit." Asmodeus pulled out of me in an instant to attend to the fire now eating one of the nightstands. He smothers the flames and looks back at me. "Look who's already manifested her element." The pride in his eyes has my heart skipping beats.

I kneel to crawl back toward him, and he backs up a half step. Now I'm hunting him. The situations so wildly reversed it gives me a giggle. I launch off the bed into his arms wrapping my legs around his waist, and he catches me effortlessly.

"We need to get that under control before you accidentally burn down our home, Love." He gestures to the wrecked end table, the leg nothing but ashes and kisses me gently. I know he's right, but I can't help my pout.

"We'll go see Lui later." He chuckled kissing my distended bottom lip. He gripped my ass bouncing me up and down a few times. "As soon as you can cum without starting a fire, we're doing this." His eyes darkened with the promise, and he set me down with a kiss to the forehead.

"Can I draw you a bath?" He asked looking weirdly hopeful. Like all he could ask for would be to put water into a tub for me to get into.

"Sure." I giggle at his excitement as he goes to run from the room, skidding to a halt just short of the door.

"Closets there," he said pointing to the only other door in the room. I shake my head, laughing as he disappears from my sight. I walk to the doors and nearly faint when I open them to realize the closet itself is an entire room. I walk into the space easily bigger than the bathroom and do a turn. Surveying the insane amount of clothes divided evenly in half, so I could tell exactly where my stuff was. Everything he got at the market was there. Shoes, belts, jewelry, accessories, down to the completely custom wardrobe. I grab a pair of basic black pants, a lace up forest green shirt and a brown leather under bust vest much like the one I wear every day. This one had daggers installed into the boning though. The hilts securely tucked into the underside, so I could easily draw them at a second's notice. How is that man even real?

I toss the clothes and a matching lace pair of undergarments the color of his eyes on the bed and shuffle to the bathroom still naked. Asmodeus was standing by the tub proudly showing off his work. Oils swirled along the water as I stepped in, and he followed suit, the tub big enough to fit us both.

"I tried to pick an oil that smells like you, but I couldn't find anything close, myrrh is a personal favorite." He bundled me up in this lap, laying his head back against the lip of the tub with a sigh, completely relaxed. The smell of myrrh and another earthy scent I couldn't place was wafting up with the steam.

"I have a smell?" I chuckled in his hold, closing my eyes.

"Like oak moss and amber and everything right in the world," he sighed. I don't think I've ever had a hot bath and I'm starting fall asleep against his chest.

"There's a lot to tell you Bryndis," he said into the silence.

"I know." I said simply, there will be time for that. I sigh, settling deeper into the arms of the man I love, and fall asleep soaking.

CHAPTER 24

Asmodeus gently lifted me from the bath, the cold air waking me from the nap I had settled into. We dress and eat quickly to set out for Lui and Libby's little cottage. As picked a matching green lace up shirt. I wonder if this is going to be a thing with him, I laugh to myself at the sweet gesture as he takes my hand. Our feet crunch through the falling leaves, the trees starting to change colors as fall settles around us.

"I know what you're supposed to have been taught." Asmodeus starts with a scowl like he personally remembered the curriculum. I guess he would have been there when it was first being written. "Do you know anything more than what you've been told?"

"Only little bits here and there about specific demons that were sighted," I reply eagerly, excited to finally have a history lesson from someone whose seen it first-hand.

"Before The Rift opened, we were in The Helscape. It's very much like this world, but their star had died, casting out all light, choking out life and leaving nothing but those who could dwell in the eternal night. Our kind arose from the destruction of that world and built a magnificent civilization. Taking advantage of those who could wield light to keep crops going with artificial sources. The strongest families were seated in territories to keep the peace, A water wielder to control the seat of each house. The royalty isn't like here, you rise to power by acts. There was no king just an assembly of lords. My father was one of them." He gave me a look, but this is probably more of the mild information I've had to adapt to. He clears his throat before starting again.

"We were multiplying quickly even with our fertility struggles and the planet we had inhabited was starting to become overrun, what little we could salvage withering. My father took it upon himself to enlist every shaman in The Helscape to attempt to open a rift to another world that we could populate and use to grow food for those that wanted to stay. It wasn't long before they succeeded landing us here in the heart of your kingdom."

"Us?' I question.

"Yes, us. My father brought me, to make sure our arrival would be a receptive one." His canines glint as he smiles, his blood wielding capabilities a vital asset, even to a king that could do the same.

"The royalty were obviously scared shitless when we showed up in the middle of their dinner. Father sat down at the table kicking his boots up and laughing in the silence. He didn't even have to hold anyone they were all just frozen. Overall, the conversation was weirdly civil. They reached an agreement, and we went back through the smaller rift to begin bringing generals over to wed to their nobility. The entire point was power, get rid of the humans in power over time until eventually everyone is just half demon or more, every single one of them answering to my father. That's when The Summits came into existence. Humans that wouldn't survive the change or bearing our offspring were matched to hopefully make stronger heirs for the next generation. Bonding a human against their will, we discovered very quickly, was significantly more gruesome than if they agreed. Regardless, anyone fit enough to even try would be matched off and whatever happens, happens." My mouth is just hanging open. They're trying to breed out humanity. And I essentially just gave mine to him? I seethe at myself for a second before realizing he was beside me, not them, and I wouldn't change my choice. I'm going to need every edge I can get to make it through this.

"The problem though, is that father dearest saw that this could be his very own little kingdom, and he wasn't going to let that slip through his fingers. King Lucifer

Morgruuth, first of his name, didn't want to have to wait the centuries it would take for you to go extinct naturally, so he opened a new rift. This one much bigger, speeding up the process of rooting humanity out by letting in the pit dwellers; those incapable of thought or feeling or reason. Essentially just releasing his hounds on the outskirts of the world. His plan worked flawlessly and now here we are years later and it's unclear just how many humans are left," he finishes just as were strolling up on the cottage. Whatever humans are left are also completely in the dark.

"I left his palace when he opened the main rift. I went to try to stop him, Lui trailing me like he was bred to. I wasn't expecting Lui to get hurt, but he was too close to the worst of it, and father did nothing as he led the charge that almost killed my friend. I got him away from The Rift and healed him myself, deciding I would never go back. I should have been causing more trouble before this though, I don't know what we're going to find when it comes to the papers they have." He gestures to the cottage.

"What if what we find is horrible?" I look at him worried. If he hasn't been back in fifteen years, there's no saying what damage has been done. What has happened to any of the human beings trapped right under the king's thumb. We'd never met someone who had been to a summit because they never return, taken to the heart of the kingdom or the cities surrounding it.

"Then we'll make him wish he never opened the rift in the first place." He kissed my nose and pulled me up the clearly fresh trail of multicolored gravel forming a walkway to the porch, Libby wasted no time adding to their little home. It had only been a day and already there were subtle and not so subtle changes to the cottage. Just little touches of Libby.

Asmodeus is knocking on the door in front of us, not letting up for a second. It was quite a few minutes before Libby emerged, stopping Asmodeus' hand mid-knock, absolutely drowning in a shirt obviously meant for Lui. Her tiny naked shoulder peeking out the neck hole as she held the fabric gathered around her, the seam of the shirt a train behind her.

"What could you possibly need already?" She was already speaking as she opened the door but stopped, staring at me slack jawed as Asmodeus brushed past her into their cottage to find his friend.

"Surprise." I waggled my fingers in an arc in front of me trying to get her to move, but she just stayed frozen, staring at me. It was easily five minutes before she thawed up, able to form a cohesive sentence.

"I'm going to put some actual clothes on and then YOU'RE ANSWERING SOME QUESTIONS." She stormed through the house, pointing at me the entire way back to their bedroom.

"'eard you're worth fightin now." Lui laughed, following Asmodeus out of the door frame Libby just disappeared into. "Told em you've always been uh hellion."

"Yeah, well, this hellion is now accidentally setting things on fire." I grin at him and the smile I receive from him is nothing short of giddy.

"Oi, this'll be a right treat." He cracked his knuckles and gestured outside already rearing to get started.

"Wait, did you find out what was being transported?" I ask him and his eyes darkened.

"Still got a ways to go lass. Let's get ya in fighting shape first." He led me from the cottage but when I glanced back at Asmodeus the shadows in his face didn't make me feel good about what little had been deciphered.

CHAPTER 25

"Shouldn't we have waited for Libby? She's going to be pissed I left without her." I eye Lui warily.

"Eh, that lil distraction will live without bein able to pry into her friends' personal lives for an hour." He chuckled; the sound warmer than I've ever heard it, And Libby said I had it bad. Lui led me off to the side, well into the cover of the trees before he made a fire appear out of thin air on some branches he dropped in a pile in front of him. He grabbed some more sticks making a second pile. The massive demon simply stood back and looked at me.

"Move it," he said, pointing to the fire with a clawed finger.

"What?" Does he expect me to pick it up? I look between him, and the small flame confused.

"Move it." He says again, just watching me, waiting. I look at the fire. It's barely burning the branches, almost as if it had gingerly been moved from somewhere else. When I would use Asmodeus' power I could feel the water around me. There's significantly less fire, so I have to really focus, searching for a feeling similar to the rushing water of Asmodeus power. I find the flame, the dancing tongues like the blood rushing through my veins. In the next blink, just like that, the fire was on the other small pile right next to it.

"Atta girl," he says, clapping me on the back; effectively knocking the wind out of me. I gasp for a second, giving him a thumbs up when he moves to check on me. He grins down at me apologetically as I finish catching my breath, hands on my knees.

"What next?" I ask once I can finally pull air into my lungs again.

"Same thing." He had me transfer that fire back and forth what felt like a billion times before he was satisfied that I was capable of moving a tiny flame ball.

"Great, now put er out," he said sitting on the trail in front of me, clearly bored.

"Why are we doing this Lui?" I ask the giant while I focus on the flame, I too am exceedingly bored and have to fight to keep the whine out of my voice.

"Doll, you just did something a hundred times it took me my entire childhood to learn. If you can get these two things figured out, you're already past the adolescent fire wielders within the kingdom. We may not have the accessibility that others have, but we are lethal when we are honed, Hellion. That means constantly aware of our sources and how to utilize them to our advantage. Your range is going to depend on you personally but I'm more worried about you being able to finish what you start." He sits back, content with his explanation. "Now, put it out."

Why would I be focusing on moving a tiny flame when I could be learning how to collect more? I feel around me, reaching out for fire and connect with a much larger well near me. I'm not sure how far, but I latch onto it, willing it to me to join the ball dancing over the bundle of twigs. The fire flared taller than Lui's standing figure, and he flew backwards rolling away from the flames before completely smothering them. He looked at me alarmed and I just grinned at him.

"I see why Lib likes you." He brushed himself off, composing himself. "I think that's enough for today," He huffed. Quickly turning on his heel to walk back for the safety of the cottage and his unhinged lover.

I laugh to myself as I stroll back, the fact that I just scared someone double my size so bad he had to run home to hide behind my best friend's skirts blowing up my ego. My first mistake was getting lost in thought completely alone in the woods, thinking about running again every day now that things are so much calmer. My second mistake was not paying close enough attention to see the person creeping behind me through the foliage. I was just about to pass the tree line for their home when everything went black.

CHAPTER 26

I awoke to throbbing in my head. I was swaying, blood thoroughly flooding my face making my vision fuzzy. I close my eyes, trying to fight the nausea churning deep in my gut. The brand on my arm burned so bad I couldn't ignore it, drowning out every other feeling in my hazy body; like it was trying to wake me up, to alert me. I fully blink open my eyes to see the ground very far below me. One of the massive demons bred to be a body-guard was carrying me slung over his shoulder.

I can't see anything past the expanse of a massive red back. Is this Lui? Did I pass out in the woods? It sounds like there are six sets of footsteps. There shouldn't be more than three. Okay, so I've been taken from the woods, again, but this time I'm not human.

So why did these ones grab me? I have no way to find out what I'm facing without getting off the shoulder of the one carrying me and there's no way to do that without alerting them that I'm awake. The brand on my arm has settled back to a dull ache now that I am fully conscious, and I try to feel for As through it. We haven't had any time to figure out how any of this works and I have no way to signal him to me, so I just hope. I hope with everything in me that he'll get the message and that my knight in shining armor will show up.

The odds aren't looking good that he'll get my beacon and I don't have the luxury of waiting. I'm not sure how long I've been out or how far we are from the cottage. I mentally feel around me, desperately trying to grab for fire in the area. I can't feel anything near me, so I branch out. I search and search and search until I find enough flame to take down the massive figure holding me in one shot. Holding my breath, I flip myself over his shoulder. The cocky idiot wasn't even attempting to hold me on, and I drop to the ground, landing on my feet. He doesn't even have time to turn before I bring a ball of fire around him so large he was instantly charred to dust, he didn't even have a chance to scream. The fire hot enough to have been borrowed from a forge.

I throw the fire up into a circular wall around me, blocking off the five remaining demons before they can get a grasp on what just happened. I can hear them shuffling, huffing along the wall, looking for a way in to grab me. The fact that they haven't found one means they probably don't have anyone capable of wielding fire with them. I can't make out their whispering over the crackle of the flame, but before I have the chance to collect my thoughts all the air whooshes from my lungs. I stand there gaping, trying to pull any bit of oxygen into my lungs. They were taking the air, Smothering the fire wall surrounding me.

My vision was starting to go spotty as I fought passing out with everything I had. When the last of the fire went out, I could see them all. A demon that looked almost exactly like Asmodeus looked me over from my place on the ground, face void of feeling, before I lost consciousness.

***

The next time my eyes open I'm on the ground leaning against a tree, thoroughly chained with the Asmodeus look alike watching me, face level with mine. The long scar running his face had to have been horrific when the injury happened.

"What do you want?" I study the calculating face of the air wielder before me, obviously a relative of my prince.

"Oh, nothing. Don't mind me, just making sure my sweet brother gets a message he will never forget." The savage grin he gives me has me struggling in the chains, but I can't get much movement. His grin has widened, and I stop thrashing to collect every drop of saliva in my mouth and spit it into his face. His grin fell immediately.

"Osroth," a gravelly voice called from behind him as he wiped his face off on the arm of his black uniform; his face not hiding his irritation at being interrupted, on top of the belligerent woman in front of him.

"There's three demons inbound. We have cause to think it's the keeper," he snivels gesturing toward me. I can't even get offended at that. My relief whooshes through me and I start laughing so hard I can barely catch my breath.

"If that's Asmodeus, I would start kissing your ass goodbye." I settled down into the ground, ready to enjoy the show.

"I'm not scared of that runt," Osroth seethed, the hatred in his eyes making my heart pang. What happened to put that hatred there?

"You should be." My laughter sobered up. Within seconds Lui landed with a crash to the ground making the earth shake, raining fire down on the demons camped out with Osroth. His arrival punctuating my words perfectly. Panicked Osroth turned, ready to smother the air from the field. He ran for his men, distracted, and I felt the metal of the chains warping around me. The links bound together becoming mangled before ending up an open mess on the ground under me.

Libby grinned out from the bushes, and I could have cried seeing that beautiful face peeking out at me. I walk right up behind Osroth, pulling one of my daggers from my vest before I kick his knees out from behind him and hold the knife to his throat.

"You should have done better research before sending your little message," I crooned down at him, holding his head back with a firm grip on the roots of his onyx hair.

Asmodeus cleared the tree line menacingly, the surviving demons around him literally exploding. He needed only call their blood forth, none of them strong enough to fight his hold on them. He was a god, and I had his enemy already on his knees in worship before him.

He studied his brother's scarred face, even his sneer was devastating. His freshly shaved face hid nothing as he stalked toward his twin. The hatred a fire burning unbridled in his black eyes, eating away the man I knew until even I feared the deity panting before me.

"You can fight us but there's nothing that you can do to stop our ascent to glory, brother. I was sent as warning. To collect collateral for the information you stole, your heart for his were his exact words I believe." My heart crumpled. They were using me as a pawn to get the information back. What we had taken was vital. So vital, the king would rank it above all else. We're never going to get another chance like this. There's no way every bit of the demon kingdom won't be locked down the second the prince doesn't return.

"I'm going to let you in on a little secret, Os." Asmodeus strolled toward him, disgusted with the thing kneeling before him. "I always saw exactly how much you needed to be liked. How much you valued the approval of swine. How their praise and attention would fuel you for weeks." He paused, his mask breaking ever so slightly as he said, "I loved you, brother."

His face hardened again as he continued, "so, every time we would spar." He stopped, watching his brother's eyes widen as he began to understand where this was going. "I always let you win." His brother barely had time for Asmodeus' words to sink in, before he exploded into bits of carnage with the rest of his band of soldiers.

Lui and Libby had already disappeared, probably going back to guard the information and I fell to my knees trembling. That was close. That was way too close. They took me out of their front yard and got us days away before they were able to catch up. I can't stop the sobs that shake my entire body as Asmodeus wraps me in his arms, stroking my hair and making soothing noises. He held me until the worst of it had passed, and I was able to look at him without tears clouding my vision.

"You came," I whispered, holding his gore specked face.

"I'll always come for you," he whispered back, kissing me sweetly. Relief courses through me. We got out of that situation just like we've gotten out of every other one. I'll train and I'll never need to wait for him to save me again, I vow to myself. Holding his face I deepen our kiss. Taking advantage of the open space, I shimmy out of my pants, kicking off my worn boots at the same time as he lifts me up backing me against a tree. He's roughly kissing me, pulling his pants down just far enough to slide into me in one movement. Trapping me between his body and the tree.

Letting out every ounce of fear we've felt over the last few days, we find our release together and a circle of trees around us lights up in a bonfire, concealing us in the center. He takes my weight in his hands as the tree at my back crumbles to dust. I look at him alarmed, but he only smiles, perfectly safe. He kisses me gently as he sets me down.

"My queen," he whispers, pressing one last kiss to my lips before pulling away to collect my blood-spattered clothes. The trail around us now nothing more than a large smoldering clearing.

"I'll explain what that was on the walk back." He eyes me, knowing I have a litany of questions. Like how he just survived the inferno I released on the surrounding trees. I nod at him, dressing quickly; and let the realization finally dawn that I've very well stumbled into the starts of a revolution.

CHAPTER 27

We started the walk home in silence, clinging to each other, wary of any small crunch in the forest. Asmodeus assured me we would be warding not only our home, but the surrounding woods. That unfortunately wouldn't help us on the road.

"Why did he seem like he hated you?" I ask, my voice small.

"Most of them do. I would side with humans. What kind of demon would oppose his kind and the natural order to help a being lower on the food chain?" He rolled his eyes. "I was noticeably favored, even as the youngest, giving everyone older than me something to prove," he said seriously. There had to be more to that story. I just stared at him. He wasn't budging though; choosing to leave whatever was there with his brother buried.

"So, your entire family is after you?" The thought makes my heart ache, my gallant prince being made their villain stoking my rage. Sparks flickered around me as I worked to regain my control. Asmodeus just stared at me wide-eyed while I breathed through the flames.

"Sorry," I said, but he just shook his head; brushing my theatrics off like they were necessary.

"Pretty much. My father has convinced them I'm after the throne, the ramifications of me leaving out of hatred were far worse than him 'banishing me.' Considering my eldest brother isn't the strongest, they were already in competition to weed each other out before I left. Each one hoping to gain fathers power and place when the void collects him."

"Have any been successful?" His family dynamic sounds like a nightmare.

"No. Not that I know of anyway, outside of me just obliterating Osroth. Now there are four." He gives a slight shudder.

"Who will be coming next?" I ask Asmodeus, knowing if they sent one sibling, they'll probably be sending another soon.

"Osroth is," he stops. "Was my twin, only older than me by minutes. If my father is trying to figure out his heir he's going to send them in order of the weakest. He'll send my sister next. Bronwyn, she wields light. I'm honestly amazed she wasn't who he sent first, if she's even alive. If not her my other sister Abaddon who wields fire, she was set to become one of the top generals in his army before I left, so she'll put up quite a fight. Considering that bonfire you just made us, she won't be a problem. Especially if we can work with you a little bit before she can get to us." His resolution was comforting but I couldn't quite be sure, not after what I had garnered of what our world looks like now. I have yet to see anyone wielding at full capacity including myself.

"Yeah, why didn't that hurt you? You should be a beautiful little pile of embers." I looked over at his completely unmarred face as my mind went back to the field; everything but a perfect circle of grass around us a smoldering ruin. My pants barely made it through unscathed, the hem of the legs singed and uneven.

"I can feel you using your power through the bond, and I was able to harness the energy and keep it away from us. Obviously not well." He gestured to the legs of my pants now slightly too short. "But we'll work together and get better," he assured me, and knowing I won't accidentally roast him one day had my swirling anxiety settling to nothing but background noise.

"So, you can't freeze me without permission now?" I give him a look, and he gives me one right back, disappointed I figured it out that quickly.

"No, I suppose not" he chuckles, squeezing my hand.

"Okay, so were going home, warding the hell out of the entire space and then just drilling until someone else tries to take me?" I ask, wanting to march down to the demons' castle right now and kick the door in myself.

"Yes, little Hellion." He said using Lui's nickname for me, gathering water balls to put out my footprints that were currently on fire behind me.

"When you're ready they will have their reckoning, and gods help them when that day comes. First our home, then your town, then the world."

I stop in my tracks. "My town?" I'm thoroughly confused looking into his angelic face.

"The people there hurt you, we will make it so they can never hurt anyone again." He strode ahead and I couldn't stop the giddiness settling deep within me. How I would love to pay Kallum a visit now that I was really something to fear. Sensing my excitement, he grinned over at me, leading the way back out of the bog.

***

We walk for a solid two days, nonstop. Our rapidly healing bodies thankfully not reliant on the sleep. I couldn't breathe easily until we were passing the wards around the outskirts of where Libby's cottage lay, specifically tuned to let us in. Lui came out to greet us, face grave.

"I think I've figured it all out and yer not gonna like it." He ushered us inside, peering into the darkness behind us, as if waiting to see the light produced from our next opponent.

Asmodeus looked through all Lui's notes as we sat in silence, waiting for him to intake and relay the information in a language me and Libby could understand. Asmodeus essentially double checking his translation. The quiet was painful, its own living entity.

"There's nearly none left," Asmodeus murmured. "The humans have almost entirely been bred out." There's a pit in my stomach as he trails off. "I don't think there's anything we can do to stop it," he says, looking at me sadly. "Nearly everyone has been moved to the heart of the kingdom." The pages he's looking at are nothing more than lists upon lists of names. Who was matched and where each couple was moved to after the summit, demons and humans alike.

"Okay, I'm confused. If the demons are being bred with the humans anyway, why does the market exist? Why is there a demand for people at all?"

"Because there aint people, Hellion. They're a soft, malleable luxury now; one that the people running those markets are going to start breeding for the price tag alone now that they've almost succeeded in wiping them out. There are plenty of sick creatures out there that enjoy breaking their toys."

"Okay, we can't save the humans, but even if we can't save humanity there has to be something we can do. There's no way everyone is willingly in their situations. There must be some way to stop it." Asmodeus stroked my face.

"This is exactly why I love you." He presses a kiss to my lips and Libby audibly gags. I gave her a look, like she isn't regularly doing much worse with her lover. She just grinned over at me, trying to quell some of my rage before I burn her cute little cottage to the ground.

"Lui, we need to train," I say to him, noticing the little singes along the floorboards that he's been putting out, subtly. I look at them both apologetically, but they just wave their hands at me, brushing me off.

"We'll train Hellion, go work off some of that rage, and we'll start when your heads a bit clearer."

CHAPTER 28

I hurl fireball after fireball at the wards, letting them catch the flame. The glimmering field around the cottage warping around the heat, forcing the fire out when it hit them.

"Careful with that, those wards can't stand forever." Lui said walking out to lead me away from the house. I immediately stop, going to apologize, but he just chuckles at me; shaking his head as he walks out into the woods. He doesn't stop until we reach a small open clearing. This time training was just me and Lui starting and putting out balls of fire until moving them from place to place and extinguishing them was second nature. I told Lui about the demon I burned to ash casually, lifting a ball of fire up in front of me to inspect it, I watch the flames dance. Noting his silence, I turn to see his eyes as wide as they would open.

"The closest forge would have been miles and miles away. How did you get that much firepower in the bogs?" He's shaking his head at me like he has something to genuinely fear.

"Maybe my range is miles and miles and miles?" I question.

"I think it is." He stared at me thoughtfully, weighing what he was about to say to me.

"Bryndis, I think you've been sent to stop this war before it can start." There's an odd weight with those words, as if I had been made specifically to forge the path ahead, for all of us; as if all the times I spent with my father picking apart our governments structure was merely the gods preparing me for the fight ahead. We continue drilling. Changing the size, shape, and intensity of the fire, learning to create and extinguish in the same breath. Once he was confident in my abilities, we started training on using the fire as a weapon. Hurtling it at people to stop them in their tracks, or wrapping it around them to incinerate them if the flame was hot enough. We practiced on various tree stumps, varying the sizes and depths. Never making the same thing twice to destroy the wood.

The days blur in a flurry of training. If Lui wasn't working with me on fire, As was drilling us with weapons. We hadn't even made it back to our home, opting to camp on the floor of the cottage. Safety in numbers and all. Libby and I were both getting decent with our short swords and my aim with a throwing knife was beyond lethal now, but blades won't do very much against a full-blooded demon outside of slowing them down. We took the time every morning to run the edge of the wards too, trying to stay as fast and agile as possible. Speed and longevity the potential difference between life and death. Our lives were a constant flurry of readying for the next attack which seemed to come right on time.

***

It had been weeks without any kind of incident. We were slowly getting stronger, and I had yet to set the woods on fire any of the few times we've been able to find some time alone. I felt capable at least, if not totally confident. First thing in the morning with the chatter of birds there was a light knock on the door. Our idle chatter abruptly stopped, forks clattering to plates. Every single one of us froze, looking back and forth at each other, trying to understand why someone would be knocking. How did they get past the wards? My stomach dropped as we all just stared at each other in silence trying to figure out what to do.

"I've got them," Asmodeus said, breaking the silence as Lui stood to open the door. Standing outside was the most beautiful woman I think I've ever seen. She was as small as Libby with golden hair that hung down her back in gentle waves. Her eyes a flood of gold much like Luis.

The impala horns rising from her curls like sun rays. She seemed to be glowing overall, from the inside out, as if she was the sun herself come down to wish us a good morning.

"Bronwyn?" Asmodeus whispers and my jaw hit the floor. This is his sister?

Her full lips opened, releasing the most melodic voice I've ever heard. "Brother." She smiled up at him warmly, regardless of the seemingly hostile demons backing him. They stared at each other in silence, each waiting for the other to speak first. Asmodeus won their stand-off.

"Father has lost control Asmodeus. Ar'un has taken over, he used The Summit as a distraction to seamlessly transfer power to himself, sealing the city into the bogs now that it has ended. Fathers plan was always distaste-ful, but Ar'un is so much worse. I don't think anyone was prepared for his plan to work and now that it has, I fear there's no stopping him." She quickly finished, her eyes pleading with my lover.

"Why are you telling me this?" He questions, studying her doll like face.

"They took Mara, paired her off with the rest at he summit. No one believes me. I don't know what foul sor-cery our brother is in league with but it's like no one has even realized father is gone," she finished, her eyes welling up with tears. The only sign of how bad it was, the disgust evident on Asmodeus face. "Please, they gave her to a human male, you can help me find her. I'll tell you everything I know, Asmodeus, I'm begging you." The plea in her voice is genuine, looking closer I notice the brand winding her arm, like the one Asmodeus gained upon completion of our bargain.

"They took your partner?" I ask, my heart breaking for the strange woman. She simply nodded, still completely frozen on the porch.

"Looks like we're going on an adventure," Libby said soberly, standing from the table to move beside Bronwyn. She pulled her gently into the cottage as Asmodeus released his hold on her muscles, rubbing a tiny hand over her back in comfort as the door shut with a thunk.

CHAPTER 29

We all moved into the cottage, crowding around Bronwyn to figure out a plan for saving her lover without having to enter the kingdom before we were ready; my fire abilities still nowhere near where they needed to be.

"Okay, so when did you last see this, Mara?" Libby sat on the floor of the still unfinished sitting room, gingerly braiding Bronwyn's long golden locks as she stared into the fire, completely lost in her own mind.

"At The Summit. Our brother called us all to be matched, since he had declared this summit would be the last. I was the only one that had caught on to what he's doing and for my silence he promised he would leave us out of his plan. I should have known he was lying. Hope is too powerful a weapon for a tyrant to leave intact." She scrunched up her perfect nose in rage that fizzled out as quickly as it came with her next breath.

"He split us like he swore to me he wouldn't, and started the process of closing the kingdom in. I barely made it out along with some of the humans who caught wind of what was happening and ran. If I had known things would have gone this way I would have spoken out. I should have spoken out." She shook her tiny head in bewilderment and Libby dropped her now competed braid.

"I didn't know where to go, so I just walked and kept walking until I ended up here. I think I was always aiming for Asmodeus; I just didn't realize," She finished. Her eyes are completely blank, like every emotion she had was dried up. She sat like that in silence, staring into the fire for a moment before she broke her own revere. "I don't think Mara is in the capital though," she whispered.

"Why not?" I ask, handing her a steaming cup of tea, sitting down cross-legged on the floor next to her, watching the flames dance upon the side of her face.

"I saw who she was given to, I was forced to watch the exchange because I fought him when he matched her. My belligerence was unheard-of, and he wanted to make sure any future acts of rebellion from me would be quashed before they could ever come to fruition." She shook her head, stomping down the few emotions that tried to break loose of the dam she had just rebuilt brick by brick. The same dam I had made for myself all those months ago.

"He was fleeing with the others, if she was with him, they would have gotten out," she nodded resolute, giving herself a small hope to hold onto; that her mate wasn't sealed inside a kingdom run by a man that would want her dead for no other reason than to prove a point.

"Can you describe him?" I lean forward slightly and placed a hand over hers, giving her a squeeze to remind her that she wasn't alone in this.

"He was huge for a human. He had silver hair, and these green eyes that held nothing but evil. The way he looked at her-" She shivered at the memory, stopping to collect herself. "He had a long scar along the side of his face." My stomach turned to lead. There was no way the universe was throwing this in my path. One of the benefits of my species being nearly extinct is the ones left are so easy to place its almost painful. I can't help the delirious laugh that burbles past my lips. Everyone just stares at me, waiting for me to explain myself, the only one slightly confused by my response Bronwyn, who still isn't used to my brand of crazy.

"It's Kallum," is all I say, and Libby's already wide red eyes light up in fury. She stands from the floor breathing heavy, a trail of expletives leaving her lips and I go to stand, trying to reach for her to calm her down, but Lui beats me to it. The ground beneath us trembles as his massive arms scoop up the now snarling, raging ball of demon. He is completely unbothered by her scratching and biting as he carries her outside to help her work off the frenzy she just put herself into.

"What was that?" Bronwyn looked back and forth between me and As. I couldn't stop the giggle that escaped me at the bewilderment written all over her angelic face.

"Just my protective best friend." The room was silent, and I can't help fidgeting with the strings of my vest, trying to come up with some way to quell the awkward energy running between the three of us.

"Why do you look nothing alike?" I ask the fire, in hopes Bronwyn or Asmodeus will answer the question that's been itching the back of my brain.

"We have different mothers," Bronwyn replied and I looked back at her, hoping for an elaboration that wouldn't come. She was just staring into the fire, the flames burning in her golden eyes as she relived the worst moments of her life. I stood from the ground pulling Asmodeus from the doorway into the kitchen to ask my questions without disturbing her vigil. I sit him down at the table, making two fresh cups of the tea I just made his sister and looked at him, expectantly. He sighed.

"In the beginning king Morgruuth had one wife. Her name is Ammit. She earned her place as his lady and now as his queen, she is very much still alive and something to be reckoned with. Demons, as you know, have always struggled with fertility. It's so bad though that we're lucky to have one baby in a lifetime; Because of this the Lords of the Realm were to take on a consort of each element, the rest was up to the gods." He finished abruptly, clearly satisfied with his explanation. I suppose it makes sense, doing what they can to even the odds, but I give him a look making it very clear I don't intend on sharing. He just laughs, shaking his head. Obviously, it's never even been a thought.

"You talk about gods, is that culture or personal?" I've never thought to ask.

"Cultural mostly. I don't know what I believe, but I don't think that this is it for us." He sits thoughtfully, pondering the question himself.

"So, having given you my soul what does that mean for me?" I've never been sure about anything other than the earth under me, not anticipating any of this.

"We use soul loosely. There's no better term for your essence in this language. It is the core of your humanity. Still a gift, but your spirit, the fire that makes you who you are is no ones to claim. I'm sure we'll have a very happy afterlife when this existence is done." He smiled gratefully as I hand him his tea with a peck to his head.

"We're going to find Mara." I say into the silence a few moments later. He looked at me questioningly, almost as if wondering if my epic powers had somehow changed to seeing the future. I huff at the thought before saying, "I know exactly where Kallum would have gone."

"Then what are we waiting for?" His savage grin had my core heating, and I shook my head at him before leaving the cabin to go find the other half of our team.

CHAPTER 30

We talk for a good chunk of the day, into the night, trying to nail down a plan. Kallum wouldn't have just walked in circles, he would have gone right back to what he knows, so they're close. Our town is only maybe a day's walk, if they're there it won't be hard to find them considering when we left for the summit our town's population decreased to thirteen.

We loaded up our packs and were leaving the cottage, ready to go help our new companion. We hadn't even reached the tree line when we saw them, easily fifty imperial soldiers lining the end of the wards. Another one of the siblings had caught up. I stood there, staring at the terror before me, thankful that the wards had just been put back up thanks to Bronwyn's timely intrusion.

The line of soldiers split to reveal a red woman, Asmodeus black eyes reflected in her face. The ends of her severe black bob brushing her strong jaw as she sneered down at us. Unlike Bronwyn this woman was absolutely shredded, packed with muscle and devastatingly gorgeous. Shorter than Lui but taller than Asmodeus, her horn topped wings extended behind her. The black uniform she wore almost sucking in the light around her. If she was trying to make a dramatic entrance she was doing one hell of a job. My knees shook slightly as she reached the ward line.

"Sister." Her eyes found Bronwyn first, her raspy voice carrying across the field with ease. A general preparing for her next battle. "I see we've joined the rabble." Her sneer intensified. A ball of fire appeared around her, and she hurled it at the wards. The fire ball dissipated to nothing. Her ghastly face came into view again, lit up by a sharp twisted smile. She started throwing ball after ball of white-hot flame at the wards, each one taking longer and longer to fizzle back out. We all started backing up, anticipating the moment the flame went through, burning a hole into the magical barrier.

"Why are you doing this? Why are you following him?" Bronwyn yelled to her sister across the field, trying to distract her. To buy time.

"I will serve the king," she replied without slowing for a second. Sweat began beading along her brow as she picked up her pace. Hurling the fire quicker and quicker, not giving the wards time to cool between blasts.

"It's not the king, you know father would never have sent you to do this. It's been fifteen years Ab," she's pleading. Knowing that when those wards fall only one side will be standing in the end.

"Did he tell you what he did to our brother?" The fire shuddered around her in time with her rage. The widening of Bronwyn's eyes the only confirmation she knew what Abaddon was talking about.

"He isn't the villain here Ab, please. We can talk about this." Bronwyn was begging her sister, tears welling up in her golden eyes.

I'm absolutely horrified, staring at the towering woman before me so close to doing something I never dreamed was possible. Dismantling a freshly laid ward with nothing but her power. Libby was working away, ensnaring guards on the ends in vines, Lui had run inside to light a fire in the hearth of the house to draw on and Asmodeus was perfectly still, sweating noticeably. I realized the only person moving was his sister. He was holding every guard in place, knowing we couldn't stop her. The only way out of this was going to be through it.

"Liar." Abaddon seethed, her rage seemed to fuel the flames itself, she was almost through.

A drop of water from the sky hit my cheek. A bad omen. I glance over at Bronwyn who's backed all the way up to the cottage trembling. Her element was light, she was essentially entirely defenseless, especially in a situation where all light has been completely choked out. The few rays of sun covered by the blackest clouds imaginable as freezing rain drops started to fall in a gentle sprinkle.

Lui exited the house, a wall of flame accompanying him just as the ward broke, the flame ball she hurtled veering off to join the wall Lui was holding firmly in front of us. Libby behind Asmodeus, is now sweating as well from the mental effort of burying demon after demon in the dirt while Asmodeus held them. She's only gotten ten in. Forty left fighting as' hold on them. I look at my friends one last time taking in every one of their features.

Abaddon parted the wall of Lui's flame, stepping through like it was no more than a curtain but Lui held it still around us. Making a full circle with us in the middle to keep any of the guards out should they break free. The smile she gave us was terrifying, nothing but pointed teeth and malice. I look back at Asmodeus. 'I love you' I mouth to him where he stands. His focus breaks as he realizes I have a plan and it's not a good one. The guards come pouring in toward the wall of fire, and he desperately tries to wrangle them all still again. The wall of flame completely blocking the field, leaving only the terrifying sounds of countless demons just outside.

Thunder cracks the sky, the drizzle turning into a pour, threatening to put the fire around us out. As focused all his energy on forcing the water away from the flame, unable to get a hold of the demons now in a jumble around the wall. I feel around for fire near me, emptying my brain the way we had done a million times now.

The wall surrounding us is so distracting I almost miss the zing through the sky. Almost.

Abaddon was working up a ball of fire from the wall itself to incinerate the people I love most. Absolutely not. I lift my hand firmly to the sky, reaching, lassoing the lightning flickering through the clouds. Using my body as a channel, I pull the electricity into me, fueling a fire so hot I can feel it crisping my system as it moves through me to jump from my other fingertips. Lines of pure lighting shoot from my hand directly at the massive demon in front of us. I hurl every bit of the power coursing through my veins out of me and into her. Her eyes widen in shock as she burns from the inside out, slowly cooking.

I let my hold drop and make sure every last bit of the scorching energy had dissipated. I felt my body, no obvious signs of damage. The smell of burning flesh was turning my stomach and I couldn't focus on the victory when the guards were still stamping around outside. Everyone looked so exhausted, but I've never felt more awake in my life. They might not have the strength to finish this, but I do. The drops are starting to hit the fire wall again with small hisses as Asmodeus' energy finally starts to run out. Bronwyn and Libby both are cradled into one of Lui's massive arms, so he can fly off with them. He grabs Asmodeus, already slumping over, in his other arm and comes for me.

"Can you hold the wall and fly?" I look into his massive face. He just stares back, knowing exactly what I'm asking. He starts to shake his head, but I look at him more firmly. "I can do this."

Asmodeus concentration fully breaks, the rain pouring onto us as Lui starts to fly away without me. As starts struggling in his massive arms trying to fight his hold and drop back down to me but its only about three wing beats before they're above the flame wall looking down at me and I'm alone. I can't hear his screams over the wind and thunder breaking the sky apart. The rain slowly dissipating the wall, the only barrier between me and forty imperial guards, trained for this exact situation.

I feel another pulse through the sky and grab onto it before the wall drops, again using my body as a conduit but this time I hold it. Letting it accumulate into me, flooding my veins with power. I give Lui a nod and right as the wall goes down, I release the fire inside of me in a full circle around me. All forty guards pacing the walls for a way in, fried in a second. Each dropping to the ground with a thud, their remains crackling and smoking.

Lui landed behind me as I fell to my knees. That one definitely hurt but it would seem I survived.

"You could have been killed." Asmodeus was pissed, shoving his way out of Lui's hold and storming toward me through the smoking remains of the field leading up to the cottage. I stood shaking my muscles out, still vibrating with the energy.

"Yes, but if I didn't try, we all would have been-" He cuts me off with a savage kiss. The desperation in it all the confirmation I needed that he knew exactly how close that was. We were incredibly out of our depth, and yet we won. His kisses take my breath away and my head is spinning when he pulls back keeping my face securely squished in his hands.

"Next time you do something dumb like that I'm gonna." But he stops. Realizing that my dumb idea saved all of us including him. He fought for words for a minute his face fluctuating between awe and annoyance. He just kissed me again, "you're a force." He finally pulled away giving me my face back, so I could survey the area around me. Making sure all my friends were good. Lui setting both girls down gently.

"It's like she didn't even know." Bronwyn said voice breaking, already retreating into herself again. No one was hurt.

"She probably didn't whinny, Ar'un isn't stupid. He's going to do everything to keep control. If she didn't know, he doesn't have fathers' power yet, unless he does, and he had just made her lofty enough promises to justify this attack." Asmodeus thoughts are spinning and so are mine. How many more of these battles will we be this lucky? We're talking about going into a hornet's nest to fight a battle it's already too late to win.

"We'll head for town tomorrow to find Kallum and Mara. I need to know how bad this is though." I look at Asmodeus, pointing a damning finger in his face. "You're translating those papers for me, exactly as they're written." I give him a glare as he tries to shake his head.

"Need I remind you what happened to the last people who crossed me, Ass?" I nearly yell at him, gesturing to the decimated field. The cottages only saving grace the wards starting just at the porch.

"I will not follow any of you blindly into a revolution. Not if people like that are what we're up against." I point to his charred sister, no longer recognizable among the bodies of her men.

He chuckled to himself, the sound humorless and nodded. We all filed back inside to regroup. Bronwyn remained silent the rest of the night, huddled in a ball next to the fire while we sat around the small table Libby had proudly but shoddily built herself.

"There are only forty-seven full-blooded humans left across the realm that were accounted for at The Summit." Asmodeus starts and I already want to throw up. Before The Rift opened there were nearly sixty thousand of us. Our civilization just starting to really take form. We had figured out indoor plumbing and electricity right before The Rift. The promise of a better future right around the bend for it all to be ruined. Taken over by a greedy man that's going to get away with it. My father must be rolling wherever his remains ended up.

The numbers were probably a little skewed, they never considered those too old or too young for the summit but there's no way we won't be going extinct and soon. That's clearly the point though if the capital has

been sealed allowing whoever is on the outside to struggle for everything. I flip the chair I'm sitting on as I stand
and stomp out of the cottage. My steps singing the little grass that's left with every step as I walk for the trees
and scream into the abyss. This can't just be it. There
must be some way to fix this. I fall to my knees, wracked
with sobs. The world I knew is gone. The world my father dreamed of is gone. The demons no better than the
men that came before them. Asmodeus' arms wrapped
around me from behind, holding me as I lose it.

"I'm so sorry, Dove. I should have done more." He was
murmuring into my hair, his lips grazing my horns. I
look up at him, the pain in his eyes matching the pain I
feel inside. There's nothing to be done for the time lost.
No way to get any of the lives lost back.

"We're going to make them pay." My tears dry up replaced by an entirely sobering, calming rage. Looking
into his face, I smile up at my prince, who smiles down
at me like he can't wait to see the havoc I'm about to unleash.

CHAPTER 31

The next morning we set out for our old town, pass-ing the bodies from the last battle still laying in the dirt. Libby skipped over them, literally spitting on the makeshift graves she formed for them as we headed back to the beginning; her savagery unmatched. My heart is ramming against my rib cage, the anxiety of re-turning home making my palms sweat. If Edna saw me like this? That would for sure be the death of her, if she even made it through the summer.

The nearly barren trees provide no distraction from the silence, each one of us absorbed in our own mael-strom of thoughts. The sun was still high in the sky when we reached Libby's old yurt. The canvas eaten into slightly after years of use, the colorful herbs had died, and the dilapidated state of her home really seemed to match where this path had led us. The Libby from our life before, just a memory. She didn't even go inside the old space, just gave Lui a nod and the canvas caught fire, burning the entirety of her past until nothing but the future remained. I sat in silence for a moment, mourning what was. Finally giving myself the room to acknowledge just how much every aspect of my life has changed, and firmly say goodbye to the past.

Her steps seemed freer as we walked further into the town. Taking the same route, we took every day to our classes. The trail was overgrown, clearly no one had used it since we left. We came upon the drive to the estate next, the ornate golden gates slightly ajar; as if beckoning us in, but I kept walking right past it, not ready to face those skeletons yet. Kallum first. We reached the main square without seeing a single other soul. The square is completely empty, the only sound the wind rustling through the trees. It was a ghost town. The few people left certainly weren't still here. Maybe he didn't come back here after all.

I circle the square where our classes used to be held, the silence ringing in my ears. I check the school building and find nothing, the professors' books I had so carefully packed still sitting where he last had them. Pulling from every fire source around me, I engulf the building in my flames. The heat fanning my hair out behind me. Asmodeus whistles and plants a kiss on my cheek as we keep walking.

I'm about to suggest just heading back the way we came when there's the sound of a scream far out in the woods to our left. Bronwyn is racing through the trees before any of us can even register what is happening, looking at each other in shock before breaking into a run after the gold streak of her hair.

"Bronwyn!" Asmodeus yells after her. I pick up my pace, pulling ahead of my friends to end up running right on her heels, right to the old hut Kallum used to live in and apparently still was.

He was standing in the doorway, holding a small demon woman by the burnt orange hair. Her golden horns glinting in the light, her arm branded with the same line as Bronwyn. She was on the ground; blood leaking from her nose, smearing across her skin, just a shade darker than her hair. The look of his face turned my insides to jelly for a second, fear trying to put me in a choke hold, when I remember the only real predator here is me.

"Is that any way to treat a lady?" I crooned at the true beast before me. It ends now, the anger, the fear, the powerlessness.

"If it was a lady maybe I would treat it better," he sneered. He clearly didn't recognize the danger he was in, choosing to ignore the face of the woman who marred him.

"A lot has changed, Kallum. Seems some things will always stay the same though." I tsk at him stepping closer and his eyes widen in realization. He backs up a step dragging the demon woman back to land on her butt with a thump. I grin at him, enjoying the terror in his eyes as my friends break the tree like behind me.

"What unholy bargain have you made, witch?" The entirety of my small group breaks out into a fit of hoots and laughter, really setting the scene for me well. Asmodeus had grabbed Bronwyn, tucking her behind him to keep her out of the way through the obvious fight brewing.

"So nice of you to join us." I turn addressing the group, making my appreciation for them obvious in my smile; though judging from Libby's widened eyes, it may not have looked as smooth as I thought. Her face was back to normal in a millisecond, giving me nothing but unflinching support in her smile back, nodding her little head at me.

"I was just about to give this one a very vital lesson in manners." I look back at his perfectly human face, smiling with cruel intent. Considering my happy smile was scary I assumed this one would be terrifying; I would have been right, his face paled.

I felt around me for fire nearby, there wasn't enough to do much damage without really reaching for it, the building fire having died down when my focus broke. There was still more than enough to make an impact. I drew the dancing tongues to me, letting the heat lick at the red tips of my hair, creating an aura of flame around myself. The heat radiating from me in a perfect arch. I take a step forward, starting a small fire in the dead grass. He takes another step back, finally dropping his hold on Mara's hair. She immediately started inching away from him toward us, moving an undetectably as possible.

"Smart girl." I hear Asmodeus murmur behind me, but my eyes are locked on the face that haunted my nightmares for years. Not ever fully understanding the weight of his betrayal until seeing it wasn't just me. Friend or foe, if it has a vagina, it's nearly worthless to him. I feel the flames swirling in my eyes and the fear so apparent on his face has me nearly giggling. He used to travel town to town so much, how many women gave him the exact same face he's giving me now?

"Run," I whisper almost too low to hear, but he's crashing through the trees away from his home. I grin at Asmodeus, who just rolls his eyes at my dramatics and gestures after my prey. Encouraging me to go catch it. Gods, I love him.

I tear through the forest after him, following the obvious trail his massive body has left. The coward. I'm smiling like a psychopath chasing this man through the woods, how the tables have turned. I let out a little laugh to myself, the sound making him pick up his pace. I've been running my entire life, he is not going to outlast me. Sure enough, the crashing stops. I approach the trail ahead. Nothing.

"Hiding?" I laugh in earnest then. If that doesn't get him going, I'm not sure what will.

"What? Are we scared of the town ogre? Didn't you know the only monsters are the ones we give power to?"

Crashing sounds to my left and I grasp a flame, hurling it at his chest. He ducks to the side, but not before I can hit a good portion of his shoulder. The clothes there melting into his flesh as he screams. It's not satisfying though. This is too quick. He's on his knees on the ground in front of me, hand shaking over his mutilated shoulder. I really thought he would be more of a fight. I scoff, the monster I've feared for so long nothing more than a fly when it came time to face me.

"Isn't that what you said when I came forward about your face? That I may look like a monster, but I would never really be anything to fear?" I looked down into his cruel face. "Someone looks a little scared right now though," I croon.

"I should have killed you when I had the chance," he seethed standing, drawing a dagger from his belt. I fully laugh in his face this time as I draw my own blades from the boning of my vest.

"You wouldn't have been strong enough, even then." I taunt him, and he launches at me. I easily duck under his blade slashing out, putting a long shallow gash across his abdomen. He curses, grabbing the shallow cut, and runs for me again. This time when I dodge, I get the other side of his face. We keep up this dance, him lunging, me cutting. When he finally slows, he's covered in little ribbons and I'm grinning at him without a scratch. He's huffing, clearly running out of the adrenaline he desperately needs to walk away from this. Oh well, I think to myself as I step forward batting his dagger away. It flies to the side, wedging straight up in the dirt. I bring my knee up into his groin, causing him to fold in half, toppling to the ground.

I take advantage of his hunched over position and give him a roundhouse kick straight to the temple, knocking him over. Somehow, he's still conscious, and reaching for the dagger I knocked into the dirt. I step on his hand and pick up his dagger. The light in his eyes dies as I stand over him, he's already resigned to his death. Well, now this is no fun.

"I thought you were going to kill me? What happened to that energy?" I taunted him from where I stood above him, still crushing his hand beneath my boot.

I bring his dagger down once to puncture his abdomen. "This is for Mara."

I bring the dagger down again, "this is for all the women I don't know about."

I bring the dagger down a final time, sliding it between his ribs right into his heart like my father taught me when the enforcers first started rolling in. "And this is for me, you sick son of a bitch."

He stopped struggling, his eyes falling to stare at nothing. I spit on his corpse and loop back toward where I exited the woods. It almost feels like I should do something, put this to rest but all I can do is stare at the body before me. The person I feared most barely more than a raindrop against my inferno. I set his body on fire. Staying to watch it burn to ash and scatter in the breeze; I stay just long enough to make sure there will never be another trace of him, before I turn on my heel and head back toward my friends. One of my monsters finally slain.

***

I find everyone exactly where I left them. Bronwyn and Mara clearly haven't left each other's arms since we found her, and I can't blame them. They all turned to look at me questioningly.

"It's taken care of." I stalk across the path to kiss Asmodeus once on the mouth. We need to find a place to stop, we need to figure out what our next steps are going to be.

"There's only one building big enough to fit all of us comfortably in the entire town." I stalk back toward the central square, time to pay a visit to Aunt Edna.

CHAPTER 32

We approach the drive once more, my heart starts to race a little bit, terrified that I'll give the frail old woman a heart attack. The idea of being her undoing puts a pit in my stomach that deepens with each step. We walk through the gates, still slightly open, the swirling gold bars growing cobwebs. It looked like they hadn't been closed since we left for The Summit. We walked further up the drive to see the door slightly ajar.

"I should have asked Kallum where everyone went," I say not really speaking to anyone, heading to the ornate gold leaf door I had opened countless times. When we walked in everything was still in its place. Like Edna had simply stepped out and forgotten to shut the door, but there was no sign of her. There is nothing but a thick layer of dust settled on the countless golden accessories lining the hearth. Everyone was so quiet.

I looked back to lock eyes with Asmodeus, whose face held all the grief I've been feeling for weeks, and all the pieces clicked together. Everyone that was left after The Summit had been rounded up. It was the last summit; everyone had a place either inside the kingdom or six feet under the dirt. Tears prick the back of my eyes. No one deserves to be herded off like cattle. It wasn't even many people; they could have let us just die out but that wasn't enough. I have to run from the house to keep from setting it on fire. My rage an inferno boiling its way out of my skin, which is exactly what it does. I combust into flames; this must be what a frenzy looks like for me.

I'm burning a path through the trees, all the way back to the main square where I put my back into throwing fireball after fireball at the rubble around the field, the cement structures not wanting to catch fire but singing under the heat with each blow. I scream up to the sky, letting the flames flow out of me in a full circle. Trying to get the pain I can't even put into words to stop. I got my happily ever after in Asmodeus and so many are suffering. Held at the whim of a tyrant. The rage is finally dying, my fire is slowly going out and I drop to my knees wracked with sobs. I curl in on myself; the guilt, anger and crushing sadness ripping its way through me. My hands, pressed to my chest, feel like the only thing keeping my heart inside my body. I'm completely naked in a field smoldering so far back I can see Edna's home.

My blast radius easily five miles at its widest point. Every bit of rubble wiped away by my flare. Everything I've ever known was a lie and now everything I've ever known has been put up in smoke. Lui only keeping the home we're hiding out in safe from the tempest of fire.

I don't know how long I sit there crying, before Asmodeus is standing over me, offering me the black lace up shirt Lui had been wearing to cover myself. As soon as I had slid the fabric over my head, he scooped me up in his arms, carrying me back to our friends to figure out what our next moves were. Pure undiluted rage was only going to get us so far.

When he set me down on the floor of the house, he scours the rooms, trying to find me some more sturdy clothing. Luckily enough, I had some stashed in my old room from before we left earlier this summer. Bronwyn and Mara have snuggled up on a fainting couch in the corner of Edna's living space, whispering to each other in a flurry of giggles. Neither meant to be on this side of a war. I shook my head looking at Asmodeus, and he stared at me like he already knew.

"I think they'll be safe here," I whisper to him. Everyone always used to call this the corner of the world for a reason, it's the last place anyone seems to stumble on. He just nods at me like he's already decided. Not that we have much choice. Our home is clearly compromised, and we're going to have to figure out how to even get into the capital. He kisses my nose as he moves to go talk with his sister. I quickly change and hand Lui back his shirt as I sit myself down beside him on the floor. Libby is firmly tucked into his lap, his back resting against the wall.

"How do you guys stand it?" I ask but the question isn't actually directed at anyone.

"What do you mean?" Lui asked, but Libby was looking at me empathetically. Like she knew exactly what I was asking.

"How do you cope with the fact that we're just pawns in a game we don't even know the rules to? How do you adjust to every aspect of your life changing with barely more than a blink?" I put my face in my hands, fingertips brushing against the spiraling horns I was still getting used to.

"You adapt," Libby said gently. "I won't lie to you and tell you that things get easier but this?" She stopped, gesturing around the room. Asmodeus now laughing with his sister, who is still clinging to her other half like she would never let her go again. "This is worth the fight. This is worth preserving." She finishes grabbing one of my hands, pulling it from my face to hold in her lap. "You were never meant to be a pawn though, Bryndis. Look outside and tell me you were meant to be anything other than the queen." We sat in silence. My thoughts whirling, so shocked at my friend's sincerity that I couldn't form words.

"You should get some sleep Bryn." Libby kissed the top of my head as she stood, pulling Lui's giant hand up with her. He ducks under the doorway following behind her.

"She's right ya know. Long live the queen." He put his fist to his chest, bowing his head to me before he disappeared from the room. I look over to meet Asmodeus eyes, nothing but approval shining there. I stand and grab his hand, leading him to the first room off the entryway. I haven't let anything that happened to me before break me and I certainly won't let this. I look into the black orbs that have been nothing but comfort for me. We'll get through this together, or we'll die trying. We seal ourselves up in the room I grew up in, fully intending to take advantage of this last night together before we head toward our probable death.

***

The next morning, we all are noticeably very weary. No one seemed to want to leave. Knowing how unlikely it would be for four people to take out an established form of government. The alternative is letting people stay stuck in the clutches of a powerful demon with something to prove. As far as we know Ar'un isn't at his full power capability yet. If we're going to make a move, now is the time. Bronwyn and Mara have made themselves scarce, and we sit at the tiny table in the kitchen area trying to get a plan.

"We need to keep training." I speak for all of us, none of us able to hold our own in our element except maybe Lui but even then, his power is limited. Asmodeus is capable of more if he works at it. He held fifty men for a prolonged period of time, theoretically those mental muscles can only go up from there.

"Our primary focus is going to have to be Ar'un and then finding father wherever he's been stashed, if he's even still on this plane. If I can get close, I know I'll win that fight, but his earth powers are unlike any I've seen."

"Yet." Libby cut him off with a pointed smile, her powers growing every single day.

"So, what? We just travel and train and hope we can make it into the kingdom?" I ask, and complete silence falls. We're discussing a revolution on the back of four people. The weight settles in, each of us nervously glancing at each other.

"Bronwyn alluded to a band of rebels that have been hiding out within the kingdom, opposing the rule of my family since the main rift opened. The only problem is she has no idea where they are or how to go about finding them." He shrugs like he has a plan.

"I'm assuming that finding them will involve some sort of grand entrance." I roll me eyes at him.

"Of course, all a cause needs is someone to rally behind, and we'll give them just that." He grinned at us; he definitely had a plan. The efficacy of it, however, was debatable.

"Their long-lost renegade prince?" I tease him.

"No, their new, powerful, previously human fire breathing queen that's the best of both worlds," He finished, grinning at me.

"Excuse me? Absolutely not," I say fuming. I didn't even know this kingdom existed less than six months ago, and now I'm supposed to be a figurehead for it.

"Bryndis, the way things have been done hasn't worked. You were given this power for a reason. I don't think we stand a chance without someone like you rallying people together," He said gently, wrapping his hand around my own. "The people that want to lead are never the people that should be leading."

"Why? Why would anyone listen to me?" My father believed in a better world. In a place where people could be free to live however they felt best, where things weren't decided at random, or for the benefit of one family.

"Because you're your fathers' daughter, but no one will ever be able to shackle you." He looked into my eyes as they filled with tears, and I knew he was right. This couldn't have all been for nothing. I can't let everything he worked for and everything he believed in die with him. We fell back into heavy silence, my mind spinning in circles over what I know needs to be done, even though I don't want to do it. "We can figure it out, power is received from the people."

"Who cares how we do it so long as we do? We have time to figure out logistics," Libby said, finally breaking the silence that had settled over us once again. "We've never been well-equipped to start a journey and so far, it's worked out well for us." She says with a shrug, and we fall back into silence again. This time collectively Brooding on our actual chances for survival.

"Come on guys! Where's your spirit? Did I hear topple the government? Gnaw at the pillars of injustice? Because I'm pretty sure that's what I heard," Libby says matter of factly, grinning up at her lover. "Is that what you heard Lui?" she bites her lip with a smile at him.

"I'd definitely say I heard sum like that, wee sprite, is that what ya heard Ass?" He says, grinning his razor-sharp grin.

"That's exactly what I heard." Asmodeus smiles. "Dove?" The three demons turn in unison toward me, sharp teeth glinting. I shrug with a sigh, there's no other choice. Outside of hiding until the world is dust, I don't see many other options. "Sounds like my kind of week." I sigh again deeply, and we start planning to travel back to the heart of the kingdom.

CHAPTER 33

We leave Aunt Edna's, Bronwyn and Mara safely tucked away into the armpit of our planet while we go to face certain death. Even knowing we don't have much of a chance to win this, I can't help being excited for the time I get to spend with my friends on the road. Our lives have been completely ruled by running and now that we're willingly headed to the place we've been running from, I feel free. Like things are finally on my own terms and I'm not just a piece being moved exactly where I'm wanted. Each of us were devoting all our mental energy to playing with our abilities as we walk back through the woods toward the kingdoms center. After traveling back and forth a few times I realized how perfectly the land slopes to their capital like one big bowl, our town in the rolling hills along the outskirts. We had spent pretty much all our time since I had met Asmodeus traveling in circle after circle, looping between the bog lands and the hills I had called home my entire life.

I'm fully prepared to be the queen in this game of chess if it keeps my friends safe, but I'd be lying if I said I hadn't been praying to every god I've ever been taught about, that a figurehead would be provided for us, so I wouldn't have a revolution on my back alone. It felt as if my training had just begun, and in some ways, I suppose it had. Yet, here i am, traveling head first into a war full of matured demons that know their world and their magic more than I could ever dream.

I don't need my hands to wield but I use them to make things easier, which in turn, gives away my moves. Lui could stand firmly in place and put a fire wherever he wanted it to go without even twitching an eye. If I could get to that point, he was pretty convinced I would be unstoppable. I have yet to be unable to find any fire when I search, even when it takes me some time. The smaller sparks I find very easily building to forging heats, like the fire is fueled by my rage alone and not the source I pull it from. His range was no more than a mile; to counteract this he always carried flint braided into a bracelet around his wrist, able to make a spark to build an inferno off of at a second's notice. Regardless of how far he is from civilization. Out of all of us Lui was the most controlled, thinking through everything before he made a move like a true general. We had been walking for a few days, now. Libby, riding on his shoulder as usual, had been growing trees, trying to improve her speed.

"What if instead of trees, you tried vines?" I thought aloud, pursing my lips as another oak popped up in a place it hadn't been moments prior. Libby had nearly gotten to growing full trees in seconds, but that would only work for so many people and going into a war, that kind of focus would be impossible. She looked at me questioning for a second and then nodded her head, flitting from Lui's shoulder on tiny wings as the ground shook, trembling violently under our feet. Brambles from the forest around us shot out from the sides of the trail to form a blockade. Completely blocking the path further into the woods.

"Like that?" she held both hands up to demonstrate her wall, smiling back at us over her shoulder, red tinged curls swinging.

"Yes, but maybe not in front of us, specifically?" I laugh at her, as her grin widens evilly. The brambles slowly retreating piece by piece into the foliage they were called from.

"Good idea though, Bryn. Entangling is a lot easier. The only problem is I can't guarantee no one will be killed in the process." She taps her tiny finger on her chin, lips pursed, figuring out how accurate she would have to be. we all just looked at her, People dying from those brambles would be an added bonus if we're up against an entire army. She giggles to herself as she re-alizes the same. Her insanity dances the border between adorable and absolutely feral. Libbys powers really were getting stronger and faster every single day; able to con-jure up anything we could possibly need from the earth, so we never needed to be separated on the trail as we traveled. Her favorite thing to do recently was to shoot vines out casually along the trail to trip Asmodeus as he walked, so focused on what he was doing she got him nearly every time, earning a fit of giggles from the curly haired imp.

As was working on how much he can hold, not want-ing a repeat of Abaddon. He didn't want to practice on people, seeing as the only people around him are friends; so he was making it a habit to make massive water ball after water ball and carry it levitating along the ground until he couldn't anymore, the ball splashing into the dirt. He was getting good. The water balls more than big enough to swallow Lui if Asmodeus wanted. He was mentally carrying them miles at a time before they splashed to the ground, and he set to work building up a new one, training his powers as if the water were weights to build up the muscles in his mind. It was def-initely working; his control was impeccable. The size of the balls of water seemed to be getting bigger each day, his ability to carry them lasting longer and longer.

As the trail began to turn swampy, Asmodeus carried a huge water ball in front of him, the biggest one he had formed yet. All of us walking behind him to avoid the splash when he inevitably drops the gallons upon gallons of water. Both Lui and Libby are so engrossed in their whispered conversation, they don't see the much smaller water ball forming behind Luis back, trailing them as they walk into the forest. Startled, I look to Asmodeus who gives me the most shit eating grin I've ever seen; he's doing this on purpose. I kept my chuckle to myself, shaking my head, knowing exactly what would come of Libby's hair getting wet.

He didn't take the warning though, and moved the smaller water ball now the size of Libby above Luis head and dropped it, completely drenching them both. Libby's red eyes only took half a second before they were raging. She immediately went wild, kicking and scratching Lui trying to get to Asmodeus; nearly diving off his shoulder at my mate right into Luis outstretched arm, already prepared to catch her. He held her back in one massive arm like she was some kind of rabid squirrel, taking the brunt of her assault. I couldn't do anything but laugh so hard I had to hold my stomach as I doubled over. My abdominal muscles straining as the giggles kept pouring out of me.

Libby stopped struggling, her frown slowly lessening as she watched me cackle. Wet hair is hanging down in her red eyes as she stares at me confused, her frenzy slowly dying. It didn't take a full second before she too started to laugh. Within minutes, we were all in hysterics. Lui and Libby both thoroughly soaked. It had been far too long since we've been able to just live like this, enjoying one another's company. I don't remember the last time any of us laughed at all, let alone with such delirious fervor. We were all laughing so hard we didn't notice the woman on the path ahead of us until she had nearly joined our party. Asmodeus' laughter died in his throat, and we all followed suit into silence as he stared at the woman before us open-mouthed and said, "Mah?"

CHAPTER 34

"Asmodeus," the blonde woman in front of us practically whispered. She looked exactly like Bronwyn, if Bronwyn's impala horns had been the color of natural bone. We all froze. Staring between the prince and one of the consorts of the king waiting, trying to figure out if this was some sort of attack.

"Is she safe?" Those three words the only ones to leave her full lips, breaking the silence. Her eyes full of a crushing sadness for her only child and the position she's been put in.

"She is." Asmodeus squared his shoulders, making himself bigger and Naahmah shrunk into herself a little bit, looking every bit the docile queen I mentally pictured when thinking of Bronwyn's mother. She's not here for a fight then.

"Bronwyn has always had a gift, never seeing the things that people wanted her to see but the truth among the lies, that was always her real power. I hoped she would have gotten out and found you. I have only heard glimmers of the hell your brother has made within the kingdom's walls from the other side of the Helscape. His transition of power happened so fast none of us could have been prepared for it."

"And what exactly were these glimmers you speak of?" Asmodeus is talking to this angelic creature in front of him like she owes him answers. Like she's not something he should fear. I take a closer look at her; She clearly wouldn't be much help in a fight, she almost looked too frail to function. Like a strong gust of wind would snap her willowy form in half, just like her daughter.

"Your brother has grown tired of waiting for the mantle to pass to him, and so he's taken it into his own hands. There's not a single lord that will back him beyond the rift, none that I've heard of from where I was anyway." Her face darkened in memory, clearly pushing past the intrusive thoughts to continue. "Your brother is weak, relying on the magic and powers of others to bolster his rule. When your father is collected by the void no one will back him as heir with all of you alive and it would only be a matter of time before they make room for a better leader for the seat of the Morgruuth house, both here and beyond the rift. If all of you are killed, leaving only him when your father does yield to the void, there will be no one to oppose his claim to the seat, not without a fight none of them are prepared for." she looked almost distraught sharing all this information, like the idea of Ar'un sitting the throne would be as catastrophic as its already seemed.

"You and your siblings seem to have played into his hand perfectly. I'm sorry you were forced into this As. If we were blessed with a scrap of humanity, it would have been found in you." Naahmah finished, somehow looking down at the man before her even though she was slightly shorter than him.

The way he was looking back at her had me questioning if he was not in some ways also her son, blood relation or not. He seemed to care what she was saying to him, the depth of her words clearly striking him. He didn't even try to put on the mask of indifference he usually turns to in these times; freely letting the tears well up in his eyes at her blatant pride in him. In that moment her golden eyes turned to land on Lui, still holding a wet Libby in his arms like a rag doll. She put her frail hand to her chest and bowed her head in respect. He did the same.

"A pleasure as always mistress." Lui fought hard to annunciate every word, making sure none of what he said to her could be jumbled. Libby wriggled out of his arm, sliding down his body to the ground, skirt trailing behind her. Ever the lady. She strode forward to offer a hand to the ethereal woman before us in an attempt to shake her hand in greeting. It took everything in me not to laugh as Naahmah placed her hand in Libby's equally tiny one to bob it up and down in a mock shake. Lui looked horrified but Libby just grinned pulling a hunk of pyrite out of her pocket, handing it to the goddess before us. Naahmah's face broke into a marvelous smile as she took Libby's rock with a gentle nod at her. Holding the rock firmly, her golden eyes landed on me.

"Mah." Asmodeus strode toward me wrapping an arm around my back to force my feet locked in fear forward. "This is Bryndis," he said simply. One arm around my back, one hand gripping my left arm just under the brand, drawing attention to it without having to shove my arm in her face.

"So subtle, Love." I rolled my eyes at him and went to give a shaky half curtsy that looked more like a bob. She smiled at me, her eyes seeing into every crevice of my being. Her gaze was light, filled with the most love I've ever seen from something deemed evil. She strode forward to wrap me in her scrawny arms, my head level with hers. She squeezed me and I wrapped my arms around her midsection, never having really given a hug like this. Naahmah merely held me for a second and kissed my cheek as she pulled away to grab my shoulders. Fully under the weight of all that love I squirm a little bit, her stare making a deep part of me ache.

"You're one of mine now," was all she said as she broke eye contact, letting me go to turn back toward Lui and Libby. I stood in shocked silence, mouth agape; my own family has never gone out of their way to claim me after the death of my father, yet here this demon was, wanting me to be a part of her family after only knowing me for a moment.

"If you're planning to overthrow Ar'un you're going to need help. I've formed connections beyond the rift, ones you will desperately need," Naahmah started. "But if I help you in this, I also need help to make sure the king is thrown back where he came from should he be found. No one being should have as much power as he's garnered for himself. There are crimes he must pay for in the Helscape, and I will no longer sit in his stead." She nodded resolutely, her eyes swirling in memory. Asmodeus was the one that spoke from behind her.

"How long have you been working against him?" He asked, bewildered.

"Since the main Rift." She said looking back at him sadly. "I realized how wrong I had been in following him here, seeing the families just like ours murdered because they weren't strong enough to defend themselves. I tried to be discreet in my work, but it became too much. I tried to speak up on behalf of the children and was sent to the Helscape as punishment for opposing him." The wheels in Asmodeus' brain were turning as he listened to her, remembering bits of his past I could only dream of.

"The time spent there was not as I had hoped, to say the least. I had no idea how deep these conspiracies he had bred ran and didn't realize I was nothing more than a body to be collateral; my presence merely something to withhold the other lords from coming for him. I managed to get away from my cell and worm my way back here just in time for your brother to seal out every being. I made it to the city gates to find no way in, and so I turned to find you. I worked with the resistance before I was forced to leave, and I worked as much as I could on the other side as well; gathering as much information as possible so when I returned, I would be backed by an army." She finished, her face hard; her intentions perfectly clear, the gods had heard my prayers and answered.

"You know where we can find this army then?" Asmodeus asked his mother figure.

"If you can get us past the wards into the city, yes." She glanced between the four of us, the silence settling, relief flooding me at her words.

"I think I have an idea," I chime into the silence, three beautiful demons and a Lui turn to me in sync, each wearing their own version of confused excitement; ready to tear the kingdom apart at its seams.

CHAPTER 35

We walk deeper and deeper into the bog, going back to the market we haven't been to in a few months now. I still need Asmodeus to carry me through the worst of it, his wielding of the surrounding water never letting him sink into the mud. I never realized that's how he did it, but as the brand tingled away it became obvious that he was solidifying the water under his feet, forcing it to carry him through the mud. The tingles are much more distinguishable now that the brand has been solidified, each burst of his power like a symphony running through my veins.

Naahmah is floating over the marshy ground, using her light as a force to keep her out of the mud, protecting her white gauzy dress and sandal clad feet. If she didn't look like an angel before, she certainly does now that she's levitating through the darkness, a beacon to the lost souls roaming these woods. Libby was sat on Lui's shoulder, whispering in his ear as we walked; making plans for when we finally reach our destination no doubt. They spent every waking second tethered to each other and every time I looked over she was mooning at the side of his massive face, completely lost in her own thoughts. The obvious love between them warmed my heart, she deserved nothing less than that happiness. The quiet around us was sobering. Outside of Libby's idle chattering in Lui's ear, none of us wanted to discuss the actual possibility of my plan and what would happen should we fail. We are all easily marked, especially the kings consort. Once we attempted this we would be hunted, regardless of if we were successful.

"We're here," Naahmah said as she gently set herself down in the more solid clearing, I almost didn't recognize it. The same clearing Asmodeus dropped me in that first day was completely different from what I remembered. What used to be an entrance into the market was nothing but a wall of vines so thick it looked to be decades old, like the base of a mountain lassoed with greenery. The gates were now sealed completely shut with vines and brambles and gods know what else. The wall seemed alive, still moving to keep its inhabitants entombed; the entire city was wrapped in them, the mismatched wooden walls covered completely. None of us had words as we stared at the monstrosity before us. Even Libby looked terrified.

"This is not of the earth." She spat toward the wall of vines which almost seemed to shiver in response. Libby's blatant disgust made my stomach turn, if it wasn't of the earth where did these vines come from? We all look at Lui, the only one of us with wings strong enough to get over the city and check it out. With a deep sigh, he set Libby down from his shoulder, kissing her on the head and launched into the skies to look for any sign of an entrance. He's gone for quite a while, the only sounds the slithering of the vines along the gates.

"What is this?" I break the silence. My thoughts whirring dangerously close to just going home and calling it quits, we could absolutely just hide out in the woods for the rest of our days and leave this for someone stronger to figure out.

"The work of a very powerful shaman," was all Asmodeus said in response, clearly all he knew.

"There are forces in play not of this world, my child." Naahmah ran a hand over my braid in a soothing motion. "We must make them relinquish their hold on this world before it is too late." Her words were anything but soothing. It's clear there would be no hiding, not if he had his hands on power like this. This dangerous game a necessity for all our survival. With perfect timing, Lui returned with a thud.

"Warded all the way around but the greens are only on the walls," he huffed, catching his breath, essentially telling us what we already knew. When we get in things were going to get messy fast and there would be no out once we broke those wards.

***

We waited by the gates for days, timing things perfectly. It was easy enough to procrastinate, knowing once we got the wards open all hell would break loose. This chance to make Naahmah the figurehead we needed, instead of bearing that mantle myself, was everything I needed to make a final plan. The only shot we would ever have of getting into this city, and taking whoever waited on the other side, was by surprise.

We camped in the trees along the outskirts of the cities entrance, worried about potentially being seen before our opportunity to strike would arise. There was nothing though. No steps in the woods, no wing beats overhead, just eerie quiet among the slithering of the vines. Even the cicadas had quieted, their roar completely stilling to nothing. Libby and Lui excused themselves to travel the trail on lookout, but given the pointed glances she had been giving him checking the trails for rogue people was the last thing on her to do list.

"Mah." I finally chimed into the quiet, the silence making me uneasy now that it was just the three of us. Her golden eyes turned to me, already crinkling in a smile, catching the light of the fire we were sat in front of.

"Yes, Love?" She was so warm in everything she did and said, the constant love radiating from her pores throwing me off.

"You were in the Helscape all this time? What is it like over there?" I could have probably asked Asmodeus but seeing as he hadn't been back in over a decade, I figured a lot of things would have changed. The way her golden eyes darkened however, had me questioning that decision.

"I wish I could tell you, but my stay was in a metal room. From what I saw going in and out the population is thriving, the sustenance from this planet serving them all well." She wasn't kidding about a cell.

"You spent ten years in a room?" I ask bewildered, not understanding how the goddess before me was caged.

"That is what I said isn't it?" She bit at me in a tone I didn't know her capable of. My eyes widened in shock and Asmodeus was immediately by my side wrapping an arm around me.

"I'm sorry, dear. My stay in our home world is a bit touchy for me," she said, completely back to normal. I lean into Asmodeus. If there's one thing I've learned in my twenty years, it's that people will show you who they are in time. First impressions usually mean very little to me, and yet I took her love at face value, assuming she would be just like her son. The man that wasn't, in fact, her son.

Naahmah excused herself and my thoughts were spinning. I looked over to Asmodeus' perfect face; he was looking at me warily, knowing exactly where my head was at like he always seemed to recently. We sat in silence for a moment longer and I watched the wheels turn in is head to figure out exactly how to phrase what he was about to say.

"Jails don't exist in the Helscape, Bryn. Not the type I'm sure you were thinking of when she had referred to her cell. Crimes against our way of life are punished in ways..." He trailed off, dancing around the truth. "That aren't very humane." His thoughts were still noticeably spinning.

"Okay, yeah, hi. You can just say it, Ass. I'm not as delicate as you seem to think." I look at his stupid beautiful face annoyed and the wheels stop spinning.

"She was tortured. For ten years she was locked in a chamber paying for the crimes my father must have committed beyond The Rift before it was opened." All the breath whooshed from my lungs, and I immediately regretted asking her for any information.

"Why wouldn't you tell me that?" I smacked his arm, fuming at how he could have let me so thoroughly eat my own foot.

"If I had known you wanted to know I could have told you, Bryn. The only difference between the kingdom in those walls-" He pointed toward the vine riddled mass just beyond the tree line. "And our home is the amount of light. When we got here our top architects replicated the conditions for our kingdom, so we would be able to settle here. Each town has a square for gatherings that are out of the cover of the trees and all the houses are built around it to keep communities' close-knit. Families usually settle together, making their own villages as they grow. Those towns are usually what a lord would rule over, the eldest in each line typically rising to power. We've made our world here. If you want to see the Helscape just look around, there is just no sunlight there to signify the days end." He gestured to the woods and my stomach was in my toes.

They changed everything about our world and their version of justice was torture. Every time I have my feet under me, I realize I still know absolutely nothing. Asmodeus kissed my cheek gently.

"We'll change things Bryn, with her help." He smiled at me, and I nodded, snuggling down into his arms. Knowing now though that she spent ten years being torn apart had me starting to second guess how well this plan was going to go, and if the woman we met on the trail a week ago, was actually the woman we were backing.

CHAPTER 36

The storm clouds came rolling in, finally, on the fourth day. The occasional drops of rain the signal that the time had come. Libby perched herself on Lui's shoulder, gripping the horn sticking out of his head next to her face with all her might as he prepared to take off. He scooped all three of us up in his arms to fly above the bubble of the wards circling the city like a dome.

Asmodeus was focused completely on my face, feeling through the brand for the slightest stirring of power to mold it around us, ideally keeping everyone from being crisped. He would help me focus my power exactly where I needed it to go. It was the only idea we had that might work, especially on something of this magnitude.

The villages furthest from the heart of the kingdom are the loyalists, or so we'd been told. Those loyal to the king were granted obscene lands and wealth to keep them quiet, so the king could keep his enemies at his heart. He chose to keep any rebels right under his nose, where they could be crushed the second they step out of line. The king had thought through everything when he established his kingdom, never making a move before success was guaranteed. Lui couldn't carry all of us that close to the heart of the kingdom, it was way too far, and then we would still have to break the wards, so facing the loyalists was our only chance to even get in.

Feeling the zing of a lightning bolt through the air I harnessed it, bringing it through my body and pushing the energy out into the wards. The lightning hit them with a boom, a small hole tearing in it just enough to let some lingering fireworks through; the sparks shooting out from the hole, raining down on the people below who had come out to inspect the noise. Screaming began as the people began fleeing the streets below, trying to find cover from whatever was exploding above them. Me.

I look around at my friends. None of them are smoking or fried so nodding, I try again. The next bolt of lightning rips the hole a little wider, the edges rippling in a glimmer but still not big enough for us to land through. The energy traveled from my body through the hole to hit the ground, charring the cement below. I needed more.

I harnessed bolt after bolt flickering through the sky until my body was humming, the fire rippling through me, sending my hair whipping out of the braid I had so carefully woven it into. The sheer power made all of us glow as I held it, aiming for the small hole I had ripped into the glimmering ward. This time, when I sent the bolt of lightning hurling into the wards, it split wide open in a flurry of sparks. The fissure spanning close to a mile as the energy buzzed along the magic keeping us out. Lui quickly landed us in the now deserted road, setting us down one by one to assess our surroundings. Every person that had been on the streets moments earlier were gone, the silence nearly deafening.

I hadn't seen where the lightning went once it had passed through the ward, the light from it blinding as it traveled into the bubble we had broken open. As I looked around, I saw stamp after stamp along the ground, the beings that had been standing there disintegrated in seconds, the power I had unleashed wiping out anyone unfortunate enough to be standing in the road. The few buildings closest to the square are standing in flames.

I gaped around me before making eye contact with Naahmah, who was looking at me like I was the key to her kingdom. My stomach turned to lead for the thousandth time this trip as I turned to Asmodeus, whose horror quickly dissolved as he took in how distraught I was. We stood in absolute silence, the crackling of the surrounding buildings the only sound. No one moved an inch, my friends gaping at me, the shock gluing us all to where we landed. We hadn't been standing there for more than a few minutes before rustling started in the canopy of trees still standing on the outskirts of this little town. The army Naahmah promised, breaking the trees ahead of us.

A hoard of demons came pouring from the foliage with crude weapons, stopping to kneel before the goddess of light next to me. Among the mass of colorful bodies, I saw humans. Full blooded people, living among the demons in the rebel army; fighting alongside them for their home. There were easily more than fifty that I could see which means the information we had wasn't correct. Clearly there were people they missed in their attempted genocide and it's turning around on them with a vengeance.

She wasn't kidding about an army, there were easily thousands of them. Men and women, demons and humans, side by side just waiting for her to breach the wards. That isn't even thinking about those who will join as we move through. The lead in my stomach lessened as I took in her army, seeing hope before me for the first time possibly ever. How did they get here so fast though? We broke the wards minutes ago, and they were already assembled and ready for her. I tried to shove my doubts aside, focusing on the fact that we may really be able to do this. Naahmah's usually soft voice was hard, carrying across the field of soldiers.

"Brothers and sisters." Her voice boomed, louder than I thought her capable of. "The time for complacency is at an end. I bring you salvation," she finished. I lassoed some of the lightning flickering through the clouds, setting it to flicker around Naahmah. Giving her the credit for the wards and the fires around us, lending her my power. She is the queen we need; she just needs to be backed by the right people. The crowd shuddered as the electricity filled the air, their bowed heads bending further under the weight of the power she seemingly held. When the lightning died, they stood as one marching in a line through the city, putting each and every building and shop that survived our landing to the torch.

"Wait, we're just going to burn everyone out?" I question, Her face hard as she looked at me.

"These homes and these businesses were bought and bound with the blood of your people. The blood of children. They must all be purified." Her blonde hair was highlighted by fire, and I stood there gaping at the woman I thought was sent from the gods not even a week ago. Her explanation was impossible to swallow as screaming rose around us, any people smart enough to stay inside through the wards breaking now trapped inside the burning buildings. My stomach dropped as the cacophony grew. Asmodeus grabbed my arm to steer me behind the army walking toward the center of the city.

"This is war, Bryn. We're going to see and do things we don't want to." Asmodeus spoke to me softly, like he didn't even believe what he was saying. Looking into his eyes I saw the swirling remorse; for the humans and his siblings and for the deaths still to come. Carrying the weight of each and every one of them on his shoulders.

"This isn't how this was supposed to go, how are we any better than them if we don't even give these people a chance to swear fealty?" I whispered to him, not wanting anyone to overhear my words as we walked, blending seamlessly into the rear of the army charging for the capital. He looked at me with those depthless black orbs and for the first time since I'd known him, he looked genuinely uncertain.

"I didn't know this was her plan. Didn't think that she would even be capable of this." He shook his head, the surrounding fires flickering in the silver of his horns.

"Will there ever be a time when we aren't completely blind?" I asked him, my voice quivering as I took in our surroundings. Every building ablaze, Libby still on Lui's shoulder ahead of us, clinging to his face through the heat enveloping us as the army pressed forward. I was so desperate to avoid having to lead that I never took the time to really look at the person that I was backing. Libby looked back at me, a fear in her eyes I've never seen before as they disappeared among the other towering forms toward the front line in search of the mad queen who had disappeared moments before.

CHAPTER 37

We burn our way through the outer cities, leaving nothing but rubble amongst the army. These pillaging's however haven't been accompanied by screaming for the most part, it was as if the shops and buildings had already been deserted. It seemed like everyone had been warned. I suppose that was entirely possible, considering we came in on a bolt of lightning. Something about the way she was moving through, burning everything in the name of justice, wasn't sitting right with me. Countless had died in the infernos, and she never batted an eye. Considering the fact that this was started because of her anger at the injustice for my people, it definitely seemed personal. I can't wrap my brain around the concept of fighting against a tyrant who tried to end an entire civilization by being exactly the same and killing innocents.

Our army was nearing seven thousand strong, quite a few demons and humans that had been hiding out within the kingdom walls had met us along the road, ready to join. The fact that they were allowed to begin marching with us with few questions, gave me hope that the senseless killing would slow once we were out of the lands of the loyalists. Things seemed far too easy. We had no problems breaking the wards and now were having no problem marching into the capital. It's as if all of this had been planned so perfectly, we need only walk to the throne and take the crown from Ar'un's head. Part of me wondered who had planned this though; if it was the queen before us, or the king sitting the throne, trying to trick us into a false sense of security. It had been nearly a week of nonstop travel and burning with nearly no sign of Lui or Libby. We never even set up actual camp, choosing to sleep along the roads as we traveled. Naamah was not wasting a moment.

We were settling down for the night, well away from the back of the army to avoid the cacophony that came every night with mealtime. She only wanted to march during the light hours, knowing most of the people we face thrive on the nocturnal schedule.

We had fallen into this weird routine of almost silence. Clinging to each other to quell the maelstrom of emotions whirling through us both. When we started this adventure none of us could have imagined the toll it would take, or the voices that would haunt us with every beat of our hearts. I settled into Asmodeus' arms as he lay back against a tree, not hungry even though it had easily been a full day since I'd last eaten. Every time I thought we were all finally on the same page, the rug was pulled from under me, and I realized just how ignorant we've always been. A ragtag band of delusional people that thought themselves heroes.

Asmodeus' breath ruffled my unbound hair as we sat together in silence. I couldn't stop the tears that started slowly trailing down my face. This wasn't how this was supposed to happen. Innocents weren't supposed to die for the vendetta of another crazed ruler. I gave her my power, let her utilize my fire to force the agenda she had decided on without a second though; naïve enough to think that the love she gave me was genuine and would be afforded to those within the kingdom's walls too. Asmodeus held me in silence as the tears kept coming, my shoulders shaking with sobs I wouldn't let break loose. I took breath after breath trying to quell the swirling in my chest. The regret nearly drowning me as it did every night we would stop to rest. My blurry vision finally started to clear as a head of reddish-brown curls came bobbing toward me. A small sandal came hurling across the field for Asmodeus' face as Liberty stomped toward us.

"What did you do?" She demanded, seething. Her other shoe already in hand to hurl at him. I broke out in a fit of giggles, drying my tears as I went to stand to greet my friend whom I hadn't seen in days. She marched right into my arms and wrapped me in a fierce hug, I could practically feel her glare at Asmodeus.

"He didn't do anything Libby; this has just been a lot." I gestured around us as I broke our hug, her little red eyes filled with understanding.

"I've been having a lot of those nights myself." She cleared her throat as her voice broke on the last word, glaring at herself for the emotion that slipped through the cracks of the wall she had built up. "I wasn't anticipating Lui becoming a main general for her. He's gone strategizing so much I wouldn't even know he was alive if it wasn't for..." She trailed off as she rubbed the brand across her forearm.

"This game is no less dangerous than the one we were talking about playing back home. At least then we were somewhat in control of our own fates though." She plopped to the ground near Asmodeus, and we all sat in a circle just looking at each other. "I wasn't kidding about you not being a pawn Bryndis," she said sadly, and I realized just how much of this could have been prevented.

"What are we going to do?" I asked into the silence but the quiet remained. None of us coming up with any way to get out of the predicament we've found ourselves in. The battles becoming something much deeper than just taking out a corrupt ruler. Every step has seemed to be intentional and it's not until it's done that we realize what the plan had been in the first place. There was still time for it to get better though, maybe Naahmah would slow as we reached the heart of the kingdom, getting past those who would oppose her.

We sat in that silence for what felt like hours as the sun set, the low light filtering through the trees that choked out the sky above us. I pulled a fire to the center of our circle, each of us huddling around it as the day gave way to night. Each so lost in our own thoughts none of us noticed Naahmah walking for us, trailed by Lui.

"I hope you are all ready for the ultimate test to our cause." Her voice broke the silence, startling us from our revere around the fire. We all stood in a hurry, and she nodded her frail head. "One of the traitors of humanity has been spotted not far from here, my armies have marched ahead to clear a space for us to disband her hold on this kingdom."

We stared at her in confusion, none of what she said was ever direct enough to fully piece together what she was saying. She seemed to always just expect those around her to follow her blindly into whatever mess she had planned for them. We glanced at each other, trying to figure out what she could possibly need from us.

"Who exactly are we facing, Mah?" Asmodeus asked carefully.

"Ammit. The queen has finally come." Her dazzling smile was terrifying. The insanity behind her eyes completely unmasked. We followed the crazed creature through the bands of men to face the queen of the realm.

CHAPTER 38

We walked up to wait in the courtyard of what was definitely once a village, every building now nothing but dust and debris. The multicolored stones under our feet swirling in a pattern I assume was imprinted on the horns of the family that had once run this small town. We hadn't been standing there for but a moment before Ammit's figure could be seen above, blocking the moon as she made to land in the courtyard we are standing in. Lui and I both set balls of flame hovering around the small space, lighting it with flickering shadows. The imp landed in front of us, her tiny purple ragged wings fluttering delicately, nothing but hatred in her eyes as she peered down her nose at us though she couldn't have been any bigger than Libby. Above small pointed black horns you could barely see in her hair, a tiny circlet of raw multicolored stones set in a stream of silver wrapped around her head, the only sign of her status among the demons. She was breathtakingly beautiful, as they all seemed to be. Her angular face perfectly proportioned under her pin straight shoulder-length black hair. Her eyes a flood of aqua blue. I'd never seen that color among any of the demons I'd been in the company of, as if the water she wielded had taken her over so thoroughly it had begun to overtake her. An ocean in barely five feet of woman. The perfect natural distraction from the predator beneath.

With her landing I lost complete control over my muscles, stiffening into a statue as she wielded my blood. I couldn't even turn my head to check on my companions, but given the complete silence I assumed they were in a similar state. I could pull a wall of flame around her at a moment's notice but Naahmah, as usual, failed to fill us in on what her plan was exactly. The imp before us smiled, the sight terrifying and even if she hadn't forced my body into submission, I would have been frozen, both in awe and terror. I had never seen someone so powerful and so at ease; as if our party was nothing for her, merely an inconvenience to be taken care of.

"Naahmah," she finally spoke, her raspy voice catching on the whisper of her name. "I'm going to be honest, I didn't know you had it in you." She grins, nothing but sharp teeth. Her gorgeous face offset by the nightmare behind her luscious lips. Naamah squares her shoulders, looking down her tiny button nose at the honed killer before her.

"There is plenty you know not of, your majesty." Her face soured as even now the title slipped past her lips. Ammit lips ticked up in the corner, pleased by the reminder of her placement.

"If you've come to stop us, I fear you've come too late." The smile Naahmah had plastered on her face was slowly slipping more and more into insanity, her cards held so closely to her chest we could all do nothing but wonder what exactly she had planned.

"I am not here for the reasons you think," Ammit said. Her smile dropped as she looked between the five of us, our army camped far behind us on mats along the trail.

"This was not what I meant to follow him to. We were meant to share this world for its sustenance, not take it for ourselves. The hierarchy in the Helscape is the way it is for a reason." She looked at our deranged queen head on before continuing. "Naahmah, you can't tell me those lords are not also starting to grow hungry. The power Lucifer has taken for himself a temptation for all. We must fix the balance before our house ceases to exist entirely."

"And how do you suggest we do that?" I pipe in, squinting my eyes as her hold on me loosens enough for me to be able to move my mouth and blink again. I'm so sick of being in the background, scared of the big bad demons around me when I'm more than capable of holding my own. It was my power that garnered Naahmah's army; and given how things were going it would be my power that won this or led to our failure.

Ammit smiled over at me, her eyes trailing from the top of my head to the tips of my toes, her gaze only momentarily catching on my brand. I squirmed a bit under her scrutiny, trying to shake off her hold on me, not used to being held like this for such a long period. She looked slowly between me and Asmodeus, still a perfect statue only steps away, smiling her sharp toothed grin.

"Oh, how interested I am in this story. Whoever was able to tame such an obstinate man must be a force to be reckoned with." She huffed out a laugh at her joke before turning back to Naahmah.

"But first we must plan. We must kill any who would stand in our way. Starting with the consorts that would back the king." Naahmah's face went blank for a moment; adjusting her plans to this unplanned intrusion before she began nodding.

"What do you propose sister?" Naahmah asked Ammit, her smile growing. As she spoke, I finally regained full control of my body, nearly falling to the ground as my muscles returned to me. she waved a hand at us, effectively dismissing us, as she walked toward the queen.

I quickly closed the distance between Asmodeus and I, using him for support as my body reawakened and we stared after the two opposing queens walking past the line of the courtyard, chattering like we hadn't come here with the intent of killing her. Confused, we all backed away heading back for the huddled masses somewhere behind us, trying to figure out what just happened and what this would mean for us going forward; but none of us daring to ask as the two disappeared beyond the burnt village in front of us. It seemed the plan would be changing yet again.

CHAPTER 39

By daybreak the two women returned, smiling wickedly, to give us a little history lesson. None of us had gotten any sleep and given the circumstances we probably wouldn't for quite some time. The main concern to our effort would be Lamashtu, who was the first of the royal consorts but not the first to bear a child. She hated children and vehemently opposed her place in the system, only accepting her role as consort to be able to fight the enemies of the king. Her hatred and apathy leading her to give her only child over to the generals to be raised amongst the war bands. Her dedication to Lucifers cause had paid off, seeing as her and her daughter both took to commanding their own legions. Both were fire wielding demons, but Lamashtu was unlike anything we had ever dealt with. This wasn't just a job to her, she delighted in the terror and pain she brought; especially that of the children, thriving on their innocence like a second form of sustenance.

There were only so many ways to bait her out of the palace, especially now that Ar'un has such a hold on so much. It would be easiest if we could get her sent out to fight the rebels quickly approaching the heart of the kingdom, but we couldn't assume she would follow the orders of the new king. Ar'un having successfully killed off all who would oppose him, but the mothers of his siblings would be looking for ways to rid himself of them too.

The lords beyond were not necessarily opposed to a woman leading if that woman would be a fit figurehead for the masses. If he's getting worried about us, he'll send her next and even if she wouldn't go for him, she would absolutely meet us to avenge her daughter; the embarrassment of her defeat something to be immediately rectified, if her history was anything to go off. We had made enough of a stir at this point to guarantee that they knew we were here, even if he somehow missed me cracking the wards open like an egg.

Ammit knew her well enough to know if we created a big enough disruption and word got back that it was Asmodeus she would insist on going alone, her pride bigger than her brain; much more like her daughter than we initially thought. So, that's exactly what we did.

We picked a city just outside the heart of the kingdom. One that had either already been picked through or evacuated and I quickly set the entire city on fire in a blazing inferno, not even needing Lui's help to get the blaze going. The crest reached the wards eating another hole through the glimmering protective barrier. Ammit had informed us that it was no secret Asmodeus was bound to an extremely powerful wielder of fire, the idea of having been followed this whole time had my stomach tied in knots.

That will get their attention, I thought to myself smugly. Ammit was just staring, wide-eyed at the destruction to my back, as I returned to the group. Keeping the inferno in its perfect circle; I smile at her smugly, making sure she saw the murder in my eyes as I walked back to my mate. He wrapped an arm around me, kissing the side of my head and I stared into Ammit's emotionless eyes as she composed her face yet again clearly shaken by the magnitude of power I had just unleashed. I may be a pawn for now but collectively we were pawns holding most of the power for the entire army.

We kept the fire still but didn't stop it from slowly dying as every building turned to ash, simply resetting the damage their kingdom had done to grow anew. There was something healing about watching that fire die and looking over the smoking remains, especially since it was a ghost town, not a single scream ringing out from the crackling inferno. The smoldering earth would one day be a field and would have trees again and life within it, the planet healing itself from a wound left by parasites. If things had to burn, at least it would one day be replaced with beauty. The mental vision of dandelions dancing in the breeze the only thing that helped me breathe through the dread swirling in my gut.

The excess was all I could see as we had traveled village to village, walking toward the capital. Each square and home was overdone in gaudy decorations that could rival Edna's home. Before being burned to ash, the richness was sickening. Every person with so much more than they could ever need, so focused on appearances that they've missed the conspiracies and genocides unfurling right under their noses. The pretty baubles around them keeping them complacent as people within their own walls suffered. I breathed in the heat as the raging fire slowly died, letting it scorch my lungs and clean out the tar that seemed to be constantly invading my soul.

It wasn't long after the fire died that mighty wing beats could be heard in the distance. We hadn't even moved our army, choosing to take this battle on with just the six of us. Ammit and Naahmah were standing in the back watching the drama unfold. The rest of us stood in a line, ready to face the monstrosity before us. Lamashtu landed on the powdered ground with a thud, her feet kicking up the thick layer of ash. She merely laughed, her sharp teeth glinting in the low light. The moon more than enough to see her perfectly.

Her strong jaw matched her daughters, black hair buzzed on the sides and a floating molten purple Mohawk above her head, her burgundy skin contrasting the neon. She was startlingly beautiful. Exactly what you would expect of the king's consort, but not of his chosen general. She was frozen in place as Ammit stomped forward, fuming at her impudence. How dare she laugh at the queen? Her aqua eyes were blazing staring at the towering demon before her.

"Oh Ammit, didn't you know?" She drawled, before Ammit could even speak, her gravelly voice causing goosebumps to break out along my skin. "I don't need my blood to wield." And before any of us could breathe, Ammit was engulfed in flames. Her screams mixing with the cackling of the abomination standing before us, delighting in her pain and our terror, finally off the very tight leash the king had clearly kept her on.

In that split second, I realized just how much danger we were in. Lui was trying to control the flames around the queen, but it was too late. Even if the flames were managed, she was gone, her screams dying within seconds. I didn't even think as I gathered every bit of fire around me, hurling it at the demon before me. It stopped centimeters short of her and her laughter increased. She pushed back on the fire, testing my grip but I didn't give her an inch, didn't leave her with even a sliver to steal from me. I took my time, fanning the fire along the wall she had built around her skin until she was wrapped in a complete cocoon. Every bit she tried to push toward us

I caught, keeping my flames completely reigned in, the towering demon before us now just a still body of fire.

"Who sent you?" I asked her. She didn't move a muscle. Didn't even breathe. I reached out for more, taking advantage of my limitless range. Slowly, I heated the cocoon encasing her, roasting the air she had managed to save for herself.

"Who sent you?" I ask again firmly, sweat popping up along my hairline as I focused on keeping my flames steady. Lui finally composed himself enough to wrap a second wall around her and contain anything that got loose.

"No one. There is no one left who has the authority to send for me. Lucifer is gone and I would sooner die than bow to that boy." She spit into the flame in front of her with a sizzle. "I will not have what we built made a mockery of," she screamed into the flames.

"As you wish," I nearly whisper as I threw every bit of my energy into shifting the flames to her skin. She was strong but I was stronger. The flames completely roasted her before she could even scream, affording her the luxury of a quicker death than she gave Ammit. She would be yet another face to haunt my dreams every night. I dropped the wall of fire looking back at Naahmah who was just standing, nodding like she had planned exactly this happening. The helplessness swirled in me as I looked at our leader. We really were just consistently a step behind her in every way, and she apparently hadn't even been here for a decade. Everyone seemed to know more, and plan accordingly but never let us in on any of it; the only reason we scrape by the gods given powers we have.

It's not only the men that have corrupted us, I think to myself grimly. I stare after the new queen as she floats back toward the army camped to the southwest. We need better. I can't be complacent in this continuing. I can't keep backing someone that would let their allies be killed for the sake of convenience. Following our group back, the complete silence is overwhelming me, strangling me in a way I didn't know was possible. There was never anything to say anymore, we were just a bunch of kids in way over our heads and there would be no way out. Not unless I made one, and fast.

CHAPTER 40

One of the many humans that had taken up residency with the army met us on the trail; bounding for us as we walked back, his frizzy orange hair bouncing with each step. I had never seen him before, but he seemed sure of himself as he walked directly up to the queen, giving a deep bow before addressing her.

"If you'll come this way, they're planning for the siege," he spoke to Naahmah only. She tilted her head down in acknowledgment and turned back for us as he left.

"We are one step closer but there is still much to do." She patted Asmodeus' shoulder and turned to walk away, leaving the four of us staring at each other bewildered. They have this entire revolution planned, and we seem to exclusively be the grunts in their war; left to do their dirty work with no say in the plans. The latest city was still smoking from the demise of someone once viewed as a goddess.

Libby looked at me worried, her tiny brows pinched together, but she said nothing; the woods around us and the army camp not a safe place to be discussing anything. We haven't had a moment to speak in what feels like an eternity, not since the night huddled around my fire. We finally made it back to Naahmah's army, breaking the tree line with a start. They had made an entire camp in the time we were gone, fully preparing for the battle ahead. We would finally have a real place to sleep for the night.

We all shepherd ourselves out of the bustle of people, into a tent erected for the prince himself, only slightly smaller than the queen's neighboring quarters. The only sign it was his, the markings on the tent flap matching the swirling in our horns. They had made quick work setting up a full compound; a tent city built right outside the heart of the kingdom.

"This is getting messy," Libby said, eyes darting between all of us. "I know I thought we had a plan, but it seems every time we step in any direction the plan changes." Even Asmodeus looked upset glancing between all of us.

"She wouldn't put us in this position without a good reason, she has to know we'll win this. Right?" Luis accent lilted through the room only to be met by silence.

She had to claw her way from the Helscape just to come back to this mess; how much would that change a person? The things she did, she did for survival, but the stains to her soul stand. Maybe we need to start making our own plans.

I look deeply at Libby and Lui. They catch on immediately and excuse themselves to clean up and get some rest before we move forward. Walking across the tent to the chair Asmodeus was sitting in, I perch myself in his lap as the flaps of the tent close behind them with a snap. His lips immediately tracing the line of my neck to meet just under my ear.

"If this is your way of trying to persuade me to go rogue, I can't say it's not working," he murmurs. I chuckle as I look over to press a kiss to his soft lips.

"I'm scared." It's all I can manage to say as his lips trail along my neck and down my shoulder. I want to take action, do something beyond play into the hands of selfish people but there's nothing I know to do. I'm just as helpless as I was as a human, even with the power gifted to me.

"Me too," he responds simply, kissing me again. Our kisses turn feverish, realizing we're finally alone for the first time in weeks. I move to straddle his lap, deepening our kiss when the flap of our tent opens. The intrusion startling me enough to nearly knock our chair over; Asmodeus catches me by the waist to keep us both from getting well acquainted with the floor. Naahmah comes floating through on a beam of light as she so often did.

"I hope I'm not interrupting," she said, breezing across the room to simply place a scroll across the table in the corner. Asmodeus fingers flexed, digging into my thighs. The small squeeze the only sign of his annoyance at the untimely interruption, before releasing them to stand with a sigh, setting me gently on my feet. I couldn't stop my glare at the back of the demon before us who had effectively stopped what little progress I had made into his pants.

Clearing his throat, he walked over to the scroll, and I stared after his muscular back, trying to equate my renegade knight with the man in front of me blindly following her orders. I could only stare as they spoke, trying to figure out how much more of this I would be able to stand for. I know it would be harder for him to go against her. She was, after all, his mother in some ways. I just needed him to see what I was seeing. That the woman he remembered isn't the woman before us and was going to gladly get every one of us killed. Naahmah folded the paper back up, handing it to him with a nod and left without another word. He turned to me smiling.

"You wanted some chaos, Little Dove? I think I have some." He handed me the paper with the blueprints to what looked to be the housing for the king's court. The only nobility allowed to live within the capital close to the king himself. These had been labeled as all his closest confidants, living in perfect little rows on top of one another, and they're being entrusted to the two of us specifically.

"Ready?" He grins at me.

"Not yet." I grin back. Jumping into his arms to tackle him to our bedroll, refusing to miss out on a single opportunity to learn every part of his body before we're sent off to die on the front lines.

CHAPTER 41

We reached the building we had been directed toward early the next morning, the sun gradually lightening what little sky could be seen through the trees. Rows upon rows upon rows of windows lined the cement walls, each window barred. Interesting. We walk into the bare bones building with ease. The entrance gave way to rows of doors meeting at a staircase in the back. We tried the doors one by one as we walked toward the stairs, each one refusing to budge. They must have barricaded themselves in, just as prepared for our arrival as the last few villages put to the torch.

We climbed the two flights of rickety stairs to reach the top level. The staircase ending with a single beaten door. Throwing his weight into it, Asmodeus crashed through the door, sending wood from around the lock splintering into the room. Brushing his shirt off and composing himself, he gave me a half smile before looking into the faint glow of the room. Surprise graced his face for only a moment before he schooled his features back into the cool indifference I had gotten so used to.

"Mother," Asmodeus drawled. Moving to circle the woman held hostage by her own blood, stepping through the doorway into a room that could have been a palace itself. The scrolling golden walls contrasted by crimsons and rich velvets. She was tucked up in a large velvet chair by the hearth in the room, a book neatly placed in her lap. She looked exactly like him. Her silver ram horns pushing through a luxurious mane of jet-black curls, her gaunt face holding the ghosts of her past. Her sunken black eyes and pale white skin were at odds with each other. A lily carried from its home pond and dropped into a lion's den.

I trail Asmodeus, taking in our surroundings, trying to figure out why the kings consort would be out of the palace. This building was close to the palace, but shouldn't she be closer to the king? Her name wasn't even on the list we were given with the blueprints. Something about this mission wasn't right. There had to be something we were missing, something the deranged queen we left behind had conveniently forgotten to mention.

"You're a monster," she spat at him; still curled up, frozen in her plush chair. His flinch was barely perceivable, but it made my stomach twist.

"Monsters are made, whatever he is, began with you," I chime in from the shadows of the doorway, stepping into the light.

"No, it began with the lying wretch we're all stuck under. Lucifer." She spat his name like it was the foulest curse she'd ever said. "I wanted no part in any of his plans." Empusa lifts her delicate nose in defiance. Not accepting a shred of the blame for what's happened to my world, to my people.

"And what makes you think you get to walk out of here when you sat by watching what he did?" I ask. I step forward, moving toward Asmodeus who was still silent. Her comment really rattled him, shaking all of the confidence from him in one breath.

"As I sat by?" she let out a forced laugh. "I have never once served the king. Not for a single moment, Child." She seethed, lost to memory. "He wanted me the second he saw me, and nothing was going to stand in his way. I came to the heart of lucifers village with my father who was petitioning for a lordship. Lucifer had already garnered enough power to be what father referred to as 'the head of the lords beyond'. My father was so desperate for power he planned to use me as a bargaining chip to gain a higher status. What he didn't anticipate was lucifer killing him to take me, no transfer of power necessary. I tried so hard to fight him, my father and Lucifer both. I didn't want a kingdom, I didn't want children, I didn't want a man." Her voice broke on the last word, the disgust in her voice evidence enough of exactly what had happened. My words catch in my throat at what she was implying, I clearly wasn't as aware to the inner workings of their family as I thought.

Their need for breeders beyond the rift had trumped their ability to love whomever they were destined to and her father, knowing that, had been ready to sell her off like cattle. He deserved the fate that befell him. Anger churned in my gut as I watched her. Her black curls were rustling, the air a breath around her; a part of her. I look over at Asmodeus who was now wide-eyed but still silent, he had moved further into the room standing to the back left of his mother's chair, so she couldn't see the thoughts turning in his brain.

"So then why are you still here?" I let my eyes flick down to her again, trying to read her response. She scoffs.

"Like he would allow me to leave? He enjoys the fight. It's a nice switch up from people bending over backwards for him. Even when he had absolutely everything it wasn't enough. I fought and raged for years and then I gave up, becoming a doll in a box when he was around, he couldn't hurt me if he couldn't touch me. It never mattered to him though. Fighting or docile, broken or whole, I will stay caged in these four walls until I wither to dust." She looked heartbroken, the silence was so loud it felt like it could swallow all of us.

"Do you not see I've never been given the choice? I sit where I'm sat, I do what I'm told, I say the things I'm meant to say. Every time I saw the sun I would run toward it, so they haven't let me see it in years." It was then I noticed the door handles turned the wrong way. She had been locked in; this room didn't even have barred windows. She had been completely sealed into her stone tomb.

This building wasn't barricaded, it was full of those problematic enough to need imprisonment but too important or entertaining to kill off for whatever reason. I had no words for the woman before me, caged and broken and left to wither away. Left to be what was needed by the man running everything. Sparks fly at my fingertips as I look at Asmodeus.

"Let her go," I almost whisper, looking back at the woman that could have easily been me if we had made it through those woods. The woman that was me even when we couldn't, trapped inside a much prettier boulder.

"But she- "

"Let her go!" I scream across the extravagant room at him. The action startling him so much he dropped his hold on her. She tentatively moved her legs, going to stand from where she was sitting.

"No more cages." I lock eyes with her. Her eyes dry and disconnected welled with tears as they met mine. I looked to Asmodeus.

"She's just another person forced into a boulder. This boulder is just gilded." I gestured to the plush fixings against the contrast of the door, pointing at the wood gouged out by her fingernail's day after day after day.

"Thank you," she uttered so quietly I almost didn't hear it and before we could process it she was gone. Flitting on the wind, nearly morphing into it as she finally escaped the cell that had been holding her for decades. Merely moved from one dimension to another like the puppet the king viewed her as. She was like the air personified, never meant to be caged or confined or minimized. Made to bear heirs for the king and be his entertainment when the perfectly willing women weren't scratching that itch.

The rage is blinding, the fire trapped within my heart coming forth, slowly overtaking the room we're standing in. The ornate wallpaper catching, spiderwebs of embers eat it away to nothing. Burning away the plush rug and chairs and countless books and paintings and every sign of the woman that was caged within. The years spent alone in between new bits of trauma forced onto her visible within those walls. I burn every centimeter of it. He would never have any piece of her ever again, no one would. Looking back at Asmodeus with a nod, room ablaze, I saw the fire reflecting the understanding in his eyes. This was just as much for me as it was for his birth giver.

Something in him seemed to settle as every bit of Empusa burned to ash, his real mother would always be

Naamah. Perhaps in some other dimension she would have been given all the children, and she would have shown them the love they deserved, and all of this would have been prevented. In another life maybe they would have all been able to just be happy, no one locked away or shut beyond the void to lose themselves. In a world without greed and lust and men's inherent need for control, destroying everything around us; but that world doesn't exist, his mother abandoned him, lost in her own trauma; his mother figure lost to a deranged insanity she could never recover from and where I came from is all but gone, humanity barely more than a memory.

This room will merely be the first. No cage will be left unopened, no bond unbroken, no person left behind to suffer the will of a tyrant. It needs to end, I'm just not sure how.

CHAPTER 42

We went through the building, door by door. We busted them in, giving the men women and children some time to collect their possessions before we could guide them to somewhere safe for the worst of what was to come. Every single person seemed frozen, almost unwilling to leave; as if they thought this was just a cruel joke. We herded the small families out. Single parents surrounded by children that had never even seen the forest unobscured by bars. The silence was damning as I burned the last of the building. Every single one of them letting the fire wash away every stain this kingdom has left on them. We watched the flames die, no chatter, no tears, nothing but healing for the families forced to live in the dark for disagreeing with the king. Their collective breath as the bars blocking each window melted away set something loose in my chest. A hope, that if we did this right, we could do other things right too. We will do better, there's no other option.

We walk back to the camp with the people we've saved, hundreds of them. Each person was welcomed with open arms by Libby and Lui. The small imp pulling packs off her mates' horns that she had hung there with care to give each family what they needed to make it through this war comfortably. They stayed at the front of the camp for hours, organizing people into the camp, so they all had their own safe space. We were apparently the only ones that didn't know these people were prisoners, if we wouldn't have taken the time to check they all would have been nothing but ash and no one would have even batted an eye, if anything it would have meant fewer mouths to feed and a blatant declaration of power. The way we've moved through the cities has given us more than enough supplies to expand our camp as needed while we finished this war, and even then, Naahmah sent us out to potentially slaughter more innocents with barely a second thought.

There is only one consort left, the mother of the man now sitting the throne. I don't anticipate this fight being an easy one, not when were actively threatening her child. Knowing Jahi would head right for the building we left ablaze, Naamah escorted Asmodeus and I back. I stole a last glance at Libby, still helping the incoming refugees, and she looked at me like it was the last time she would see me; her mouth open to yell something our way before she was swept up in the flood of people, her curls lost in the shuffle.

I followed them but couldn't stop the pit forming in my stomach. We usually faced people with better odds than this, even when it was just us traveling through the woods. It's almost as if the further in we get Naahmah is testing us, seeing exactly how much we can handle without being crushed. We wait by the ruins of the jail. The concrete still smoking from the holes that used to be windows, the bars melted in puddles along the walls, glinting in the light. The next closest building is the palace itself; if the trees wouldn't have been so dense we probably would have been able to see it in the distance.

The earth rumbled, the plates under us shifting to open around us, the only sign Jahi was coming. We each set to work dodging fissures in the ground opening to swallow us. We should have brought Libby, I thought panicked as the ground beneath me began to open and I jumped out of the way, falling onto my hip right before I could be swallowed by the earth. We still couldn't even see her beyond the ruins. I quickly jumped to my feet, looking over to Asmodeus who was completely still, focused on holding her and drawing her out to us, so we could see who we were even fighting.

She came stepping around the building clumsily, like she was fighting Asmodeus' hold with everything in herself, her rage bolstering her power. Before I can process anything about the woman in front of us, I'm being pulled into the dirt. Vines wrapped around my ankles in delicate loops dragging me into a fissure in the ground. Using my fire, I burn away the vines, but they're popping up again too quickly, gaining on me every time until I'm wrapped in them mostly up to my waist. The thin brown strands of earth digging into my skin as they encircled me. Asmodeus' head was whipping between me and Naahmah, looking at her pleadingly, trying to figure out what he was supposed to do and why she was standing back just watching this unfold. Jahi had stilled now that she was in our range of sight but her blood being controlled by Asmodeus didn't stop the earth from trembling beneath us.

I was up to my chest in dirt, still trying to burn away the vines as Asmodeus started trying to pull her blood from her, attempting to end her the same way he did his brother. She wasn't giving him an inch. He was panicking, I was panicking, only Naahmah stood firmly behind us as if nothing was happening. We were losing faster than I even had time to process what was happening, I couldn't even get a good look at the demon we were facing, too busy trying to dig myself out of the hole she was pulling me into. Buried up to my neck, I was choking on dirt as Naamah sighed heavily over us, shaking her head. I looked up, seeing the glimmer of stars through the leaves overhead. At least if I had to die my last sight would be a beautiful one and not one of carnage and destruction, like everything we'd been encountering for weeks now.

Looking at Jahi, Naahmah twitched her eyebrow and the woman exploded in light. Every orifice of her body lit up, burning from the inside out as if a star had been placed at her center. The light went out, and she dropped to the ground dead, her corpse smoking from her burnt out eye sockets. All I could really see was the moon above us, my face the only thing still sticking from the dirt. I began frantically clawing my way out of my grave, sputtering as I met Asmodeus' arms who ripped me the rest of the way out of the vines.

"What the fuck was that?!" He screamed at his mother figure, holding me in shaking arms. Stroking his hands over my hair and down my back trying to assure himself that I was okay. The light touches were welcome as my stomach churned and I fought with everything in me to keep what little food I had eaten where it belonged.

"I needed to know how strong you are. I needed to know if you would be able to overpower someone regardless of element. I must say I'm quite disappointed. I expected more from you." She was looking right at me as she spoke, before she turned away to walk back for the army we had left behind. I stared at her gaping. She was willing to let me be buried to test how strong I was?

"I can't rely on the weak to win me my kingdom. I must plan," she said over her shoulder not even deigning to look back at us, leaving us staring after her in shocked silence. We didn't have much of a plan going into this, but I couldn't have anticipated for a second that this was where we would end up.

Pressing a gentle kiss to my lips in reassurance he holds my face as we stare into each other's eyes and the course has never been clearer. She's no better than lucifer or Ar'un or any of the disgusting rulers that came before them. The gravity of what just happened hit me like a truck in that moment and I ripped my face from his hands to retch over the nearest tree. The adrenaline leaving my system, nothing but shock left behind with each heave. I fall to my knees, hands to the ground as the contents of my stomach empty and Asmodeus strokes my back; murmuring comforting words to me as the betrayal worked its way out of my system through my mouth, but there was nothing he could say that would fix this. There was no way to ensure we would survive this. She had been capable of that the entire time and never once stepped in to help us. We were completely fucked.

Tears streamed down my face as Asmodeus scooped me up to carry me back to camp in silence. What was there to say? We were in too deep, there was no way to get out of this, or away from the person that could summon stars from the sky.

CHAPTER 43

The army was already prepared to depart when we got back. Libby ran to me, throwing her arms around my mid-section.

"I was so worried," she whispered into my now empty stomach. She pulled back looking up at me, checking for injuries. She had wrung her hands raw waiting for us to return.

"This isn't right," I whisper to Libby, and she gives me a sharp look silencing my thoughts. She feverishly glances around before nodding at the both of us. Lui was nowhere to be seen as we took our positions among the tail of Naahma's people. She was nothing if not a showman and wanted to make an entrance. The army marching for the gates was meant to be a distraction as we sneak into the palace in search of Ar'un. The goal was to minimize bloodshed as much as possible, likely to placate the masses. Ultimately all Naahmah cares about is the throne, not the blood coating the ground to get to it. Lui was meant to fly us in, but we were greeted by a green demon similar in size. His mottled flesh stirring memories of far unluckier demons that had crossed our paths.

"Where is Lui?" Libby said firmly as the demon reached forward to bring her into his arms. She bared her teeth at him, batting his hand away and my stomach dropped a bit. The plan had changed and although it didn't seem like much now, I'm sure there was more up her sleeve than what we were seeing on the surface.

"By her majesty's side as requested." We all looked at each other, Libby's face crumpled. Looking at her now, she seemed almost like her old self, just a small lost angel trying to skate by unnoticed. Naahmah was meant to be with us and yet here we were, loaded up in an unfamiliar males' arms flying toward the palace through the night sky. This was just another game she's decided to play without filling any of us in on the rules. Clearly our failure meant more than we even realized.

We knew where we were meant to go, the palace drawn out on maps in each of our backpacks in case any of us get turned around. This seems like a distraction though. Why is Lui needed with her? And then it hit me. With him we were too powerful, if he is by her side she can use him as collateral for us to relinquish the throne should one of us reach it first, knowing now that on my own I'm not unbeatable. Not only that, but he was the quickest fire wielder I've ever met, she kept who she deemed the most powerful by her side and sent us off to either get her the throne or die in the process. This entire time it's all been about the power, why would it suddenly change now? She's seen exactly what our power combined is capable of, and she chose her setting for this final battle accordingly.

Libby was glaring over at me. Not at me, past my body toward the army marching with a demon of light at their front. More than likely hovering ahead like a goddess when she was nothing more than a snake. The displays of power she's made publicly have all been mine, bolstering her, her hands only getting dirty when we failed to defeat her fellow consort. She could have stopped this at any time, easily the most powerful wielder of light imaginable; but she chose to sit back and watch as me and my friends killed countless people in test after test leading us up to this final trial.

The green demon was slowing, discreetly flying us through the dark, into the palace gates, landing in the stables next to the servant's entrance. I couldn't stop my jaw from dropping at the sight of the palace before me. The black slabs of River stone melded together with metal. Iridescent veins matching the flow of water from centuries past. The early dawn light illuminating the walls, catching the flowing silver.

We walked along the palace in the total silence. Every person that should have been manning the grounds are focused on the commotion at the gates. Grabbing Libby's and Asmodeus' hands, I start walking toward the door we were told to go into. Libby pulls back for just a second, looking toward the gates as if she could see her partner marching on the front lines.

"We'll get him back, Libby." I pulled her arm, moving her toward the door with us, but I wasn't confident. We were just much more likely to get caught out in the open than in the servant's halls.

"Yeah." She replied, but her whisper came out broken. I didn't allow myself to dwell in her terror, we had to do this, the only way out is through; especially now that were in the enemies keep with only the three of us and our wits to get us through. Libby's fear wasn't easily ignored though, I hadn't seen her this scared even before she transformed and given the circumstances of our last battle, I'm really in no position to be reassuring her. She was almost hidden behind us as we traveled the dark walkway. Her curls shaking as she walked, as if all her confidence had been funneled out of her and kept at Lui's side. I stopped abruptly pulling them to a stop with me and just looked at her, her tiny hand holding her stomach like she was about to throw up.

"You say the word, and we will walk right back out of here, Lib." I whisper to her in the cover of the darkness.

"We aren't going to walk back out of here," She responded simply. Libby took a deep breath, quelling her fear and kept walking toward the throne room, dropping my hand. "We'll be the ones to end this, Bryndis. No more games." She spoke over her shoulder as she walked.

The pit in my stomach deepened at her words, knowing just how true they probably were. We weren't on the front lines, but we also definitely weren't the key players, expendable as we've always been. I have to fight to keep the fire in my veins within me as we reach the door we're meant to go through. Taking a deep breath, Asmodeus nudged the wooden door open, letting us in on a dais to the right of the throne. The mixture of wood and metals looked like a tree had pulled the minerals from the earth around it to make a perfect raised seat. The high back ingrained with a swirling pattern so close to Asmodeus' horns I stopped to do a double take of it. As if the seat had been made for him. Practically Reading my thoughts he mumbled almost too softly to hear.

"For the king."

The throne room was empty. The silence deafening as we moved into the room toward the seat, footsteps ringing through the open space. A blood-red runner ran from the massive double doors at the front, all the way to the stairs under the throne. The crimson a river running through the black stone under our feet, the entire palace made one slab with silver reinforcing each crack and crevice. Asmodeus just stared at it. The genocide, the pain, the games. All for a stupid chair. All for the power that comes with it.

"Well, well, well." A deep timbre rumbled behind us as the ground under us began to shake. "I think that seat's a bit big for you, Little Brother." The ground crackled underneath us, the stone flooring parting to let in the vines from outside.

Libby held them firmly, keeping them from wrapping around us, choking the life from them with her rage alone. "I've been waiting for this." He smiled broadly as he stepped into the room from the enormous double doors. He was massive, a mountain of a man himself and I couldn't stop my slight tremble as I fully took him in. Ar'un looked at the dead vines at our feet and then at Liberty who was looking at him with a feral rage I had only seen just before she went into a frenzy. She was completely still as she stared him down, a killing calm settling over her.

"This will be such fun," he chuckled. Muscles bulged under his orange skin as he cracked his knuckles. No more running, this is exactly what we came here for. It is finally time to face Ar'un.

CHAPTER 44

The ground rumbled with each step he took into the room. He was easily bigger than Lui, a giant with a buzzed head and black antlers shooting to the sky. His head and chest were covered in scrolling ink that glowed a sickly green, the characters etched into his skin giving off a dark energy I could feel across the room. He had tapped into something dark to make this happen, his morals abandoned for the sake of power. Libby wasted no time. Shooting vines out to wrap around him, hitting him with each one as he focused on trying to catch any of us in the snares he was rapidly shooting through the fissures in the floor. It was a dance, and we seemed to be winning it, none of us even touched by the greenery while Libby's vines had left welts across his exposed chest and biceps. He seemed to be laughing through it though, as if the pain was nothing more than a feather brushing against his skin.

"Is that really all you have to offer?" He chuckled at my tiny friend and her face scrunched up in fury. He had stopped moving, Asmodeus holding him still and I wrapped a wall of fire around him; encircling him, so he couldn't see where he was aiming. He tsked behind my wall.

"Is that supposed to stop me, Bryndis?" We all stopped, completely still, he knew more than we thought. The only sound was the crackling fire, each of us holding our breath.

"What have you done Ar'un?" Asmodeus called out; his voice pained. He had lost his entire family through this; my world wasn't the only one that has ceased to exist.

"I've gained infinite power, brother. There is nothing and no one safe from my reach, and all I needed to gain all this control was just the blood of a king." His laughter turned hysterical beyond my wall of fire and my stomach began turning.

"Well, a king and quite a few powerful subjects. You would be surprised what a shaman is capable of achieving with the right incentive." The abandoned towns hadn't been abandoned but sacrificed in the name of the new king. In a breath, shadows gathered, a deep black mist choking out the sunlight starting to filter through the large windows. The entity surrounding us, putting out the fire wall I had made around him, stifling everything but the green glow coming from the characters etched into his flesh. We were frozen, staring at the man in front of us that was no longer a man at all but the epitome of evil.

The fire hadn't even been out for a second before Libby let out a pained scream, a thorned vine wrapping around her ankle and calf pulling her over to crack her shoulder against the stone of the floor. The second her scream rung through the air it was matched by a deafening roar as the room was enveloped in fire. Every piece of earth in front of us was burned away as Lui came charging into the room, tackling the bigger demon to the ground. We were all unscathed by the fire, but the blast of heat was enough to blow my hair back. Naahmah was still nowhere to be seen. He must have followed their bond, tracing her to the fight we were currently facing.

Asmodeus held Ar'un in place as Lui pummeled him, fists flying into his face over and over and over again. I started reaching, collecting fire to use against him, the shock finally wearing off enough for me to focus. Lui pulled the motionless demon to his feet and backed up as the fire accumulated in a wall around them that I slowly began moving in, wrapping it firmly around Ar'un's body. He struggled against Asmodeus hold but every bit of movement he gained was pushing him into our fire. The earth trembled, and I was trembling too, trying to finish him before he could unleash whatever hell he was growing for us beneath the stone floors.

Lui joined my struggle, the fire moving quicker and more efficiently than when he had been beating the king. We pushed, both of us with all our might until the flames were licking his skin, his form barely visible inside the flames. The swirling black mist he had summoned was trying to put out the fire around him but with both of us holding it and drawing in more he couldn't break our wall. With a roar the ground shook one last time before there was silence. The fire completely wrapping around him to burn him to ash, leaving nothing behind.

As the fire died, I looked around me. Everything seemed to be moving in slow motion, my brain physically incapable of taking in any more information, after the past few months. My heartbeat was pounding in my ears as I took in my surroundings. I looked over to Asmodeus, who was on his knees screaming but I couldn't hear him past the steady thump of my heart. Following his gaze, I saw Lui's massive form. He was completely impaled by a tree from the ground sprouting through his body and out his neck, his head hanging at an unnatural angle to the side. I could only stare mouth agape at the gruesome scene before me. There was no coming back from that type of injury, no matter how advanced our healing abilities were. He was gone before I even saw his body.

"Never to be apart again." Libby's voice echoed through my mind and all of a sudden everything was moving again. Asmodeus was screaming and our flames were crackling. I whipped around to find my friend, still on the floor behind me, her fragile hand over the area on her neck the tree was exiting Lui. She was so still, barely breathing against the intrusion that wasn't actually there. I ran across the room skidding to a stop on my knees by her body, wrapping her frail body up in my arms.

"We can fix this Libby, just hold on." I was rocking frantically, holding her to me; trying to get Asmodeus' attention to help me, but he had walked over in a daze and was trying to break the tree out of his friend's body piece by piece.

"I can fix this." My voice broke. The tears falling from both our eyes said otherwise. She shook her little head at me, reaching her hand up to brush my hair back out of my eyes, trailing her fingers over where her daisy circlets would always fall on my head.

"Don't keep me from him." My tears started falling in earnest, she wouldn't want to live without him, even if there was a way around this. "Make it count Bryn," She whispered up at me. "Me and Lui will be waiting for you." She smiled sadly at me.

"I can't do this without you. Please don't leave me." I sobbed into her tiny hand.

"You'll never have to, I promise." She smiled up at me, her face lighting up one last time, a final dazzling gift before her light was completely extinguished. The silence was going to swallow me whole, my ears are ringing with it as I hold the frail body of my best friend.

Naahmah chose that moment to finally make her appearance, not saying a word as she crossed the room to mount the throne triumphant; sitting herself on it like she belonged there. The fire in my veins let loose, my breath coming in strangled gasps that barely sounded like breaths. Spiderwebs of embers crawled along Libby's skin, slowly turning her to ash, the more I tried to stop them the faster they picked up until there was nothing left of my friend but the crystal she had been holding since we started our march this morning. My sobs were frantic as I took in the ruby, identical in color to Lui's skin. Without even meaning to she was gone in an instant, her body scattering in ashes along the stone floor. I took deep breaths trying to calm the inferno boiling just under my skin as I look directly at Naahmah, sitting, smiling on her throne.

"You did this." I seethed from my kneeling position, the heat escaping me swirling my hair around my shoulders, the band holding it back in its usual braid had busted sometime during our fight. My rage was all consuming, lifting me from the ground to hover in the air. I point a damning finger down at her and my skin erupted into pure flame. This frenzy so calm and collected it barely even felt like a frenzy, I was fully in control this time. It was judgment day, and I was the executioner.

Her eyes widened and I felt the tiniest burn from the light she was trying to hurl at me. Day had broken now though, and she couldn't pluck any stars from the sky to hurt me like she hurt Jahi. A critical miscalculation on her part. The sun was far too intense a being to be har-nessed, its power blocking her from the help she desper-ately needed. There would be no more senseless killing, no more games, no more plots; just my fire as I ended the woman who stole all that was left of my old life.

"You don't deserve that throne." My voice is flame it-self, carried by the wind to burn away every impurity be-fore me. "No one does."

The palace erupted. Magma shot through the fissures in the floor consuming the room around us. Naahmah couldn't even blink before she was eaten by the lava, my anguish personified in flowing waves of fire. Asmodeus was shielded in a perfect bubble keeping the fire away from him, curled up in a ball on his side in the exact spot the corpse of his friend once was. I let the fire cleanse the palace, leaving nothing but scourged earth. Every single one of them needed to be destroyed, not even a whisper of them left on this world. I put every bit of pain and heartache from every second of my life into bringing this kingdom to its knees. I would not play their games anymore, I would not sit idly back and watch countless people suffer because it suited those in charge. It ends, and I'll be the one to end it. In this mo-ment I wasn't a queen, I was a goddess.

The palace melted around us, the metals and river rock slowly disintegrating into an island until the magma journeyed back through the ground to where it came from, sealing itself back up under the melted carnage of what I'm sure was once an exquisite palace.

Standing in my destruction I looked to Asmodeus, who couldn't seem to do anything more than move to me to wrap me up in his arms as we both let the pain go.

We were crying into each other, dropping to our knees as we used the others body as an anchor to our world that has been destroyed so thoroughly it would never be the same. The emotions we had been holding in for months finally coming out in a tidal wave that took my breath with it.

"What now?" I look up at Asmodeus after what felt like hours, unable to shed any more tears.

"Now we make it count, Dove." With a deep breath he kissed my nose, before turning to address the masses that had accumulated around the slab, staring wordlessly at the destruction we had rendered. Now we make it count, I thought to myself but could feel nothing but emptiness as I watched Asmodeus lead like he had always been meant to.

CHAPTER 45

W e decided immediately that there would be no more kings, Asmodeus only took charge as much as he absolutely had to. we needed to band together to build anew. We left the palace a heap of molten rock on the ground to commemorate the destruction of our world. There is nothing we can do to change the past, just rebuild for the future. The middle of the bog lands would still definitely be the best place to settle, the low light making it comfortable for everyone around the clock even if they didn't want to thrive on the typical nocturnal schedule.

Things started slow. Little huts and buildings popping up neatly around the slab that used to be the palace, making it a new square of sorts to form our new world around. There were so few of us now, Naahmah's army disbanding with the disappearance of their queen, happy enough with the way things had ended to head back to rebuild their own lives. Each wielder using his or her powers accordingly to help their neighbors rebuild their homes. Some of the people we had rescued from that concrete jail were actually smiling, their hope radiating from their pores as they built.

I completely poured myself into making a new city, often forgetting to eat as we built building after building for the families displaced. The army wandering through the cities before the siege did a good job of picking off our enemies and those that would put any of the men or women we found back in a cage. We haven't had any incidents, really. We seem to just be a group of extremely relieved people trying our best to rebuild from the ground up.

I haven't given myself any time to think, only allowing myself the space to work and sleep, curled up in a bag beside Asmodeus on the marshy ground. I haven't spoken, and he's made no attempt to either. It's as if the light we both held simultaneously went out and there was nothing either of us could do about it. Every night I see her face, smiling up at me and every morning I wake with the knowledge that once these dreams fade, I will never see that face again. Not in this life. I startle out of my usual Libby dream, this one drifting into a nightmare. Asmodeus laid next to me, staring sadly down at the top of my head when he also should have been asleep.

"We need to talk about it, Bryn." I shake my head at him vigorously but can't stop the tears welling in my eyes.

"She knew something was wrong, I should have listened, and we should have gone back," I say voice wobbling. It's the first time in days I think I've actually strung words together, my voice hoarse from disuse and the tears settling in my sinuses.

"There's nothing we could have done differently, Dove. If we had turned around, we would have just been trapped under someone else's thumb. She knew what she was giving going into that last battle, and she gave it willingly so that we might be able to fix the things they couldn't. We still have to figure out ties to the Helscape and how to get them sustenance, so all of this wasn't for nothing. We don't have the luxury of stopping life. We have to move on, move forward. For them. We have to live double the life, so they didn't give everything in vain." His eyes were welling up too as he stroked my face gently, he was right.

I pressed a kiss onto his lips as the sun rose above us, the start of another day since the end. He had clearly been thinking about this just as much as I had over the last few days since our world shattered. He was right, living a shell of a life isn't what Libby would have wanted for me.

I stood from the sack we've been sleeping in, offering my hand down to him. With a small smile, my prince took it and rose next to me to walk to the main square to pick up where construction left off. We walked, hands interlocked, ready to grab materials for the next home when my breath was stolen from my lungs as we reached the clearing.

The slab in the center of the square was covered with the smallest vines, spanning the entire stretch of molten rock. From those vines sprouted a field of tiny daisies, as if Libby had heard me and answered in kind; still backing me wherever she was. Looking at the field I squeeze As' hand. We would make it count. We would build a better world.

For them.

ACKNOWLEDGMENTS

Wow, where to even start. Writing this book has been one of the most intense whirlwinds I've ever experienced in my life and I'm just so insanely grateful.

To my husband, thank you so much for being so patient with me as I wrote non-stop for weeks at a time and giving me all the space I needed to get this story out.

To my children, thank you for your never ending grace and the constant writing breaks to look at the art you completed right alongside me.

To Mckenna thank you for seeing the potential in this story and helping me to see it too. Ivy, thank you for letting me constantly pick your brain and taking the time at a whim to read snippets and make sure I was headed the direction I wanted.

To Lena and Connor thank you for your unwavering love, support and excitement. You both reignited my fire every time it started to waver and I appreciate you more than I have words for.

To Kyla and Kevin, thank you for everything. For consistently taking the time to help me succeed in whatever ways you could, for all the late nights helping me figure out technology and believing in meeven when I felt like I couldn't do it and for designing some of the coolest cover art of all time.

And finally to my best friend Jasmine. You have been the biggest rock for me and my favorite person to bounce my ideas off of. Thank you for loving me and loving my characters. Your belief in me has changed my life.

I have received so much unwavering support and I genuinely don't have words for how much I love and appreciate each and every one of you. Thank you for supporting, thank you for being there, and most importantly thank you for reading.

SNEAK PEEK

**Read on for a sneak peak of the connecting novella
coming 2025**

LIBBY

The woods are blurring around me as the demon holding my hair drags me through the brush, strands ripping out in the process. I should be in pain, or trying to get away but all I can think about is my friend who will be clearing the tree line of our camp any minute now just to find that I'm not there anymore, if she hasn't already. I stopped struggling after the first hour of being dragged, the grip on my hair unwavering as it pulled me across the spongy ground, further into the darkness. My flailing was doing nothing but hurting me further.

So here I sat, arms folded over each other as this stupid green imp ran over the ground pulling me behind it. It had to drop me at some point. I was small, but the slithering creature holding me was much smaller and would have to get tired eventually. As soon as I could stand and see what I was doing I could stomp its minuscule, little head in. This was no different from any of the countless snakes that would slither along our garden back home. Those I would let pass by peacefully, but those don't grab my hair in a death grip and drag me into what I can only assume is their home. If this thing is planning to eat me it's going to have one hell of a time.

I scowl at the sky peeking through the canopy of trees. Bryn is going to lose it.

The stars are glinting above me and are really all I can see in the inky forest around me as I go bumping along the ground, the crystals I wove into my curls clattering together, ringing in my ears. We stop with a jerk, the grip on my hair lessening just enough for me to shake it off and jump up, whirling to kick at the thing that just stole me from my best friend. The thing that had grabbed me had completely vanished. I turned in a half circle, surveying the trail I was on but I could barely see in the blackness. My eye catches on something moving in the distance, all I could see was a slight shift.

Squinting my eyes, I started to walk forward on the trail before halting abruptly, remembering where I am. Whatever was moving could come to me. The shifting became more pronounced as it got closer and closer. Now maybe fifty feet away I could see that what I was looking at was a massive pair of burgundy legs. I barely came up to the hip of the creature before me and my heart started to pound as I took in the massive form slowly making its way right for me. The disembodied legs are all I can see from the distance I am at, and I am not about to stay here waiting for it to catch up. Fumbling backwards not able to take my eyes off it, I hustled back in the direction I had been dragged from, taking in the towering form before me as more and more started to come into view. A sculpted chest I wish I had the time to appreciate joined the legs, all I could see of its face were massive oxen horns above glowing golden orbs that looked down on me menacingly.

My heart raced frantically and all at once it stopped. My skin igniting in a blaze that scared me more than whatever was approaching me. I was on fire, engulfed in imaginary flames singing every single nerve ending. I dropped to the ground trying desperately to roll the fire off my body, but it wasn't wrapped around me, it was inside of me. As the burn quelled, I cracked my eyes open from the ground. The pain couldn't have lasted more than a minute and my confusion was overwhelming as I looked around, realizing my surroundings were suddenly bright as daylight. I squint against the onslaught of light to let my eyes readjust. The sun hadn't risen but I could see every mote of dust drifting through the air in front of me. I didn't have time to stare in wonder at the sights before me as I locked onto those golden orbs floating a good four feet above me. The massive burgundy demon was terrifying, nothing but sharp teeth and malice. My entire body began quaking. I couldn't see a way out of this or away from him and I'm not going down without a fight.

Looking dead in those golden orbs I charged at him, heading directly for his legs which shockingly folded under the weight of my body as I launched into them. He rolled back bringing me with him, but I never gave him a chance to grab me, scurrying up his body to claw at him ferociously. I may not survive this, but I'm done with being defenseless. I will not go into the void docilely. Bryn isn't here to save me; I'm going to save myself, so I can go back for her, or at the very least rid this plane of something that could hurt her. If I'm going down this thing is going down with me, that girl that would cower is dead.

He stood, arms whirring, trying to catch me as I climbed up his body heading for his head to try to crack that massive skull. That seemed to be a theme in demon killing in the classes we were forced to take. The only way to kill the bigger ones was going for the head. I was too fast for him and I mounted his shoulders with ease, grabbing at his head but I severely underestimated the size difference and my stupid tiny hands couldn't grip his massive head. I put all my weight into a jump back, pushing his shoulders forward as I went flipping off him, dropping to the ground. There was a crack that rung through the air before my feet could plant and I tried desperately to reorient myself. My head stopped spinning right in time to see the massive demon firmly lodged into a tree on the trail. His horns dug so deep into the bark he couldn't seem to pull them out. The growl rippling from his body made my heart, pounding again, slow down. He was terrifying but the fear had my body doing some very weird things. The reverberations racing to mingle in my core in a way I don't think anything ever has. His massive hands were pushing against the tree, and I almost felt bad for what I had done to him. From this view I could see his massive horn tipped wings, unfurled to help leverage him so he could rip his horns from the tree, but he didn't seem to be budging.

His muscled back had my mouth watering slightly and I realized I had been chewing on my lip. I shook my head viciously, trying to clear my thoughts. This thing would eat me if given the chance and I should be running but I stood there, just staring at him struggle, wondering how those claws would feel brushing along my skin. I realized with a start I had gone from biting my lip to gaping at the thing in front of me, and not even in shock. My face burned as I turned to walk away, but he was still stuck and I couldn't just leave him there defenseless, could I? He hadn't attacked me, I attacked him and there's nothing to say he would have if I hadn't charged at him. My thoughts were at war with themselves. I didn't have any time to make a real decision as he ripped his head sideways, pulling his horns through the bark, gauging the trunk of the tree thoroughly.

He turned on me with a grin that was bordering on feral, making my toes curl in my boots. I wanted so desperately to be as scared as I was moments before, but I couldn't. He was weirdly cute. His scrunched-up face only becoming nightmare fuel when I got an eye full of razor-sharp teeth but something about them had my stomach twisting in a good way. I had always been very different, never having a crush on any of the boys or girls in our town and I always thought it was because of the limited options, but I'm realizing now it was because I was apparently attracted to something very different. He strode toward me menacingly, but I held my ground, craning my neck to look up and meet those golden eyes.

"I like the cut uh yur gib." He said, his accented voice so deep I could feel it in my bones when he spoke, and I had to suppress a shiver. I needed to find my friend but maybe I could recruit this massive bad ass in front of me to tag along. I was so lost in my thoughts; I almost missed the last part of his sentence.

"I think I'll be keeping you." He nearly growled and my eyes flew open, my trance broken as he reached down with one massive hand, wrapping it completely around my waist to lift me up closer to his face. A massive split tongue peeked out of his mouth to run over his teeth, and I couldn't stop the shiver that raced down my spine at the idea of what else that tongue could run over. I almost slapped myself, trying to shake off the increasingly inappropriate thoughts. He said he'd keep me?

"I'm not some docile little pet you can find in the woods and bring home to mommy." I glared at him, and his eyebrows rocketed up in genuine surprise.

"oi. I'm counting on that." His grin of razors lit up his face as his wings began to beat, his feet leaving the ground. He was taking me somewhere, probably further from where I needed to be. The only thing I could think of was my best friend somewhere behind me, less than a day away. Her blue eyes with a spot of brown in them framed by black and red hair at the forefront of my mind. With a deep breath I began my fight again, kicking and clawing and refusing to let this brute take me where he wanted without a struggle, even though every part of me wanted to see exactly what he had planned.

ABOUT THE AUTHOR

A.N Frederick is a native Floridian and stay at home mom to four littles. Three of them started school this year and with that extra snippet of freedom she chose to write a book. Her hobbies include eating novels in a single sitting, baking her anxiety away, prowling her local renaissance festivals, deep diving into true crime and spending time adventuring with her favorite humans. Her love of romantasy and insane intake of books have her wheels constantly turning and so while Bryndis is her first published work it will be followed by many more. For more information about upcoming books visit her website.

www.anfrederick.com